FAMILY MONEY

OTHER TITLES BY CHAD ZUNKER

DAVID ADAMS SERIES

An Equal Justice
An Unequal Defense
Runaway Justice

SAM CALLAHAN SERIES

The Tracker
Shadow Shepherd
Hunt the Lion

PRAISE FOR CHAD ZUNKER

An Equal Justice

HARPER LEE PRIZE FOR LEGAL FICTION FINALIST

"A deftly crafted legal thriller of a novel by an author with a genuine knack for a reader-engaging narrative storytelling style."

—Midwest Book Review

"A gripping thriller with a heart, *An Equal Justice* hits the ground running . . . The chapters flew by, with surprises aplenty and taut writing. A highly recommended read that introduces a lawyer with legs."

—Crime Thriller Hound

"In *An Equal Justice*, author Chad Zunker crafts a riveting legal thriller . . . *An Equal Justice* not only plunges readers into murder and conspiracy involving wealthy power players, but also immerses us in the crisis of homelessness in our country."

—*The Big Thrill*

"A thriller with a message. A pleasure to read. Twists I didn't see coming. I read it in one sitting."

—Robert Dugoni, #1 Amazon Charts bestselling author of *My Sister's Grave*

"Taut, suspenseful, and action-packed, with a hero you can root for. Zunker has hit it out of the park with this one."

—Victor Methos, bestselling author of *The Neon Lawyer*

An Unequal Defense

"In Zunker's solid sequel to 2019's *An Equal Justice*, Zunker . . . sustains a disciplined focus on plot and character. John Grisham fans will appreciate this familiar but effective tale."

—*Publishers Weekly*

Runaway Justice

"[In the] engrossing third mystery featuring attorney David Adams . . . Zunker gives heart and hope to his characters. There are no lulls in this satisfying story of a young runaway in trouble."

—*Publishers Weekly*

The Tracker

"A gritty, compelling, and altogether engrossing novel that reads as if ripped from the headlines. I couldn't turn the pages fast enough. Chad Zunker is the real deal."

—Christopher Reich, *New York Times* bestselling author of *Numbered Account* and *Rules of Deception*

"*Good Will Hunting* meets *The Bourne Identity*."

—Fred Burton, *New York Times* bestselling author of *Under Fire*

FAMILY MONEY

A THRILLER

CHAD ZUNKER
AUTHOR OF *THE TRACKER*

THOMAS & MERCER

Text copyright © 2022 by Chad Zunker
All rights reserved.

Published by Thomas & Mercer, Seattle

www.apub.com

Amazon, the Amazon logo, and Thomas & Mercer are trademarks of Amazon.com, Inc., or its affiliates.

ISBN-13: 9781542026161
ISBN-10: 1542026164

Cover design by Shasti O'Leary Soudant

Printed in the United States of America

To Doug, my father-in-law,
for your unwavering faith in me.

No Lies, Ever

ONE

The first thing that struck me as odd when my father-in-law was abducted right in front of me was the calm look on his face. Joe did not appear to be shocked when three young Mexican men suddenly jumped out of a run-down gray minivan and grabbed him in the middle of a small village eight miles outside of Matamoros. He did not yell out to me, "Alex! Help!" Instead, Joe just kind of stared at me with a resigned expression from across the crowded outdoor marketplace as they began yanking him backward toward the vehicle.

Yes, he fought them—at first. Joe did not go easy. His lean arms thrashed against their pulling. My father-in-law was in great shape for being in his late fifties. He still played a lot of golf and tennis. Joe had no trouble keeping up with me on our runs together on the downtown trail back in Austin. But he was no match for these muscle-bound men who wore dirty T-shirts, jeans, and boots. They looked more like day laborers than organized criminals. Two of the men secured Joe by the arms. When the biggest of the group grabbed his legs and lifted, the struggle was basically over.

With a heavy sack of groceries clutched in my arms, I hesitated a moment, squinting across the vendor tables against the blinding glare of the late-afternoon sun. What the hell was happening? Were these men really dragging my father-in-law away? I flashed on the conversation I'd had with Taylor—Joe's only daughter and my wife—about a month ago when we'd first talked about taking this trip. Taylor had been concerned about bringing our whole family down here to assist at an orphanage. She'd read so many horror stories about kidnappings and other violent crime on this side of the border. My wife always researched everything to death and then usually focused on worst-case scenarios. It drove me crazy. I tended to be the simple idealist. I had assured her we would be perfectly safe. We would only be twenty miles south of the border. We wouldn't even be spending the night inside Mexico; instead, we'd stay at a Holiday Inn in Brownsville and cross over the border each day.

I'd had a friend who'd recently brought his own family down to the orphanage and said it was a wonderful experience, especially for his kids. This had also been true for us thus far. Our young daughters, Olivia and Nicole, had loved being with the other children this week. For the past five days, they'd done hundreds of crafts together, played games, put on plays, and kicked the soccer ball around for countless hours. I'd never seen my girls smile so much. While the kids played, Taylor, Joe, my mother-in-law, Carol, and I had rolled up our sleeves to put fresh coats of bright paint on dingy walls of various bedrooms inside the old two-story building. Joe and I had left the orphanage an hour ago to drive over to the nearest village and buy groceries for dinner tonight, as we'd done several times the past week. My mother-in-law wanted to make a special vegetable-and-beef stew for all the kids. An old family recipe from her grandmother. My kids would usually devour it.

Everything about this trip had been a dream—until now.

I cursed, dropped the sack of groceries, ran toward the van. Unlike Joe, I was already in full-on panic. I weaved around other outdoor shoppers, who all turned to stare at the frantically sprinting thirty-two-year-old white man wearing a paint-stained orange Texas Longhorns T-shirt, tan cargo shorts, and flip-flops. A small boy pulling a rusty red wagon suddenly stepped out in front of me. I tried to leap clean over him, but the toe of my flip-flop caught the wagon's edge. I toppled face-first onto the ground.

Scrambling to my feet, I ran forward again while spitting clumps of dirt from my mouth. The men now had Joe fully inside the minivan. Again, my father-in-law held my gaze. Staring directly at me through the open door, he mouthed something.

I'm sorry.

Was that what Joe had just said to me? Why would he say that?

One of the men pulled a black hood completely over his head. I felt my stomach twist at the sight. Then another guy yanked the minivan door shut. I reached the vehicle just as the tires began to spin and kick pebbles of gravel up into the air. I grabbed the outside door handle, yanked on it several times, but it wouldn't budge. Pounding on the side of the minivan, I began yelling, "Wait! Please stop! I can pay you. *Dinero!* I'll pay right now!"

But the driver of the minivan only sped up. I ran alongside it for maybe fifty feet before it was going too fast for me to keep up. I tried to jump onto the back of the vehicle but couldn't find anything to grab. I lost my balance, fell onto the dirt road, and rolled several times, my flip-flops flying off my feet in different directions.

Again, I pushed myself up, looked all around for another way to stop this nightmare from happening. My Chevy Tahoe was parked on the other side of the marketplace. By the time I got back to it, the minivan would be long gone. I needed help ASAP. I glanced over at a host of pensive faces staring back at me. A lot of villagers were milling about and watching things unfold. None of them looked shocked by what had just happened.

I ran straight up to an older man wearing coveralls with a gray beard. "Please help me! *Policía! Policía!* Please!"

He nodded. *"Sí, sí."*

He snapped his fingers at a teenager who was standing next to him. The kid punched on his cell phone, lifted it to his mouth, and began speaking rapidly in Spanish. I didn't know enough of the language to understand what all he was saying, but I hoped he was talking to the police.

The teenager hung up, looked at me. *"Diez minutos."*

"What?"

"Policía. Diez minutos."

"Ten minutes?" I snapped.

I knew enough Spanish to understand that. I'd practiced the basics with Nicole and Olivia leading up to the trip. I wanted them to be able to communicate on some level with the kids at the orphanage. For a five-year-old and a seven-year-old, they had a knack for grasping the language. Both of them were really smart girls. They got that from their mother.

I again thought of Taylor, felt my chest tighten up. Ten minutes was a lifetime. I couldn't just stand there and wait for the police. I spun around, stared back at the crowd of onlookers in the marketplace behind me. Could any of them help me? Did anyone know these men who had grabbed Joe?

"Habla inglés?" I began repeating, going from person to person.

All I got back were blank stares and shaking heads. Did no one here really know how to speak English? Most looked like poor people who'd probably never traveled too far away from this village. But then I noticed one Mexican man near the back of the crowd who stood out from the others. Clean-shaven with slicked-back black hair, he was probably my age and wore a nice gray suit with a white dress shirt unbuttoned to midchest. I doubted he was a local villager. Maybe he could help me.

I made a move in his direction. When I did, he immediately turned and slipped away into the crowd. I quickly lost sight of him. I cursed again, stepped back into the dirt road, stared off into the distance. All I could see now were big clouds of dust circling up under the blazing heat of the sun. I fell to my knees on the dirt. My hands were trembling. I kept seeing that black hood being forced over my father-in-law's head.

Joe was gone. I couldn't stop it.

What would I tell my mother-in-law?

What would I say to my kids?

How could I even face Taylor?

God, please.

TWO

I paced in a furious circle right in the spot where my father-in-law had been grabbed and had a hard time catching my breath. My heart was racing. I kept reliving every detail of the abduction like a horror film looped in my mind. Who were those guys? Why had they chosen Joe? And why had he not looked as panicked about it as I had? I knew my father-in-law to be cool under pressure, but this was not the simple stress of him making an argument in a courtroom trial. This might be life and death.

I checked the time on my phone. About five minutes had passed since the minivan had disappeared, but it felt like forever. Where were the damn police already? The village was only eight miles outside of Matamoros. It shouldn't take someone ten minutes to get over here. A few concerned bystanders continued to stare at me with tight faces, but most others just went back to business as usual in the marketplace. Did they see this kind of thing all the time?

A barefoot young girl of probably nine wearing a yellow sundress walked up to me and held out her hand. I looked down and noticed a familiar-looking cell phone in her tiny fingers. I recognized it right away as Joe's phone. It must've fallen from his pocket in the struggle. The phone had a white case with *Papa* printed on it, the name surrounded by pink-and-purple butterflies. Olivia had designed it using one of those online gift stores and had given it to Joe as a birthday present last year. I remembered laughing out loud. It wasn't exactly the manliest-looking phone case. But my father-in-law told her it was the best birthday gift ever and didn't hesitate to place it on his phone. Joe adored his two grandkids and would do anything to make them happy. He would regularly play day spa with them and let them do his hair, nails, and makeup. He would even participate in their cute little plays and wear whatever costumes they dreamed up for him. Joe's whole life was his family.

I took the phone from the girl. *"Gracias."*

She gave me a small smile and ran off.

My own phone buzzed. I held it up and saw a text from Taylor.

Hey, babe, what's your ETA? Getting hungry around here.

I felt my throat catch. How should I respond? I couldn't tell her about this over the phone. I had to be there with her in person.

A second text arrived from Taylor. A heart emoji along with a photo of our girls playing dress-up with three similar-age girls from the orphanage. Olivia and Nicole had insisted on bringing an entire duffel bag filled with their Disney Princess outfits. They'd made good use out of them this week. I had a feeling we'd be leaving the costumes behind for the kids at the orphanage and buying all new ones when we got back to Austin.

Looking at Taylor's second text nearly brought me to my knees again. I had talked her into coming here. I had created this nightmare. One she didn't even know about yet. I already felt my heart breaking at having to tell her this news. If we didn't get Joe back, would she ever forgive me? Would I ever forgive myself? How had this happened? Just a few hours earlier, we were the happiest family you could find anywhere, splashing around together in the hotel pool. The day had started perfectly, but then everything had unraveled on me so fast.

"We really need to go, Alex," Taylor had said to me that morning, frowning while she stared down at me in the water from the edge of the hotel pool. "I told them we'd be there by ten."

Taylor and I had been together sixteen years—ten married—and she still took my breath away. Even while wearing plain jeans, running shoes, a simple white T-shirt, her brunette hair in a ponytail, and very little makeup.

"Come on, Mom!" shouted Olivia. "Five more minutes!"

"Please, Mom, please!" echoed Nicole.

Both girls were splashing around in the shallow end of the pool next to me in their cute pink-and-purple matching swimsuits.

"Yeah, Mom, don't be such a party pooper." This came from Joe, who was also in the pool with us. We'd been taking turns throwing the girls as high as we could and watching them shriek with absolute joy.

"Don't encourage them, Dad," Taylor said, rolling her eyes.

"Where's the fun in that?" he replied with a wide smile.

We'd had the hotel pool to ourselves. It wasn't much. This wasn't a luxury resort. But we were making the most of it.

"We have time, babe," I said to Taylor, wading over closer to her.

"But we have to pick up paint supplies, remember?"

"That's true."

I heard more squeals from behind me, turned. Joe had launched Nicole into the air again, and she'd done a little cannonball into the water. She'd been working on perfecting her cannonballs in our pool back in Austin. She was so proud of them, even though her tiny splash barely rippled more than a couple of feet.

She popped up out of the water, the biggest smile on her face. "How was that, Papa? Was that even bigger than last time?"

Joe's eyes lit up. "It was huge!"

"My turn! My turn!" yelled Olivia, swimming over to Joe.

My mother-in-law walked out to the pool area toward us. Carol was tan and trim with short brown hair. She played tennis in a senior league three times a week. She and Joe had been married thirty-two years. They'd wanted more kids, but Joe told me complications during Taylor's birth had prevented that. So our family of four was all they had. Our lives were completely wrapped up in theirs, too. My in-laws lived only two blocks over from us. While most sons-in-law might be wary of living so close to their in-laws, I welcomed it. Joe was a mentor to me in every way. Carol was of great help to Taylor with the kids. She was readily available without being overly intrusive. And my girls adored Papa and Nanny, as they liked to be called.

Carol stood next to Taylor, crossed her arms. "What's going on out here?"

"Dad's being a troublemaker again," Taylor said.

"Of course he is. Joe, we really need to get moving, honey."

"All right, all right," Joe relented. "Sorry, girls, playtime is over."

Joe climbed the pool steps, found his towel on a patio chair, and began drying off. Carol walked over to the steps and helped the girls out while I searched the bottom of the pool for their swim toys. I collected them all, moved back to the side of the pool, and held them up for Taylor. She reached down and grabbed them with both hands. When she did, I quickly slipped my right hand around and clutched her wrist. A small grin touched my lips. Taylor's green eyes flashed on mine.

"Don't . . . you . . . dare," she warned me, trying to pull back.

But I didn't let go. My grin began to spread.

"Alex!" she said.

This caught the attention of our girls. "Do it, Daddy! Do it!"

I saw a hint of a smile on Taylor's face. I knew this was the permission I needed. So I yanked her all the way forward on top of me into the pool. Coming up out of the water, Taylor tried to frown but couldn't stop herself from smiling. The girls were exploding with laughter on the patio. There was nothing better than hearing unbridled glee coming out of both of our angels.

The next thing I knew, Joe had scooped up Carol in both arms and was running toward the pool with my screeching mother-in-law. They both splashed into the water right next to us. Then Olivia and Nicole jumped back into the pool right behind them, and soon we were all laughing so hard, our stomachs hurt.

Taylor gave me a kiss. "Babe, I'm so glad you talked me into coming on this trip. It really has been a wonderful week for all of us."

"Thanks for trusting me."

The last thing I'd said to her this morning in the pool now felt like a dagger jabbing hard into my ribs. Thankfully, I spotted a blue Ford truck with *Policía—Matamoros* on the side finally pull up to the marketplace. A uniformed officer probably in his forties with a crew cut and a thick mustache got out. I hurried over to him.

"Please tell me you speak English," I said.

He nodded. "Yes. And you are?"

"Alex Mahan."

"Officer Sanchez. But call me Raul. Tell me what happened, Alex."

"My father-in-law and I were shopping here in the village when some men grabbed him. We've been helping out over at a nearby orphanage this week—Casa de Esperanza."

"I know it well. The director, Esther, is a friend."

"Well, I was standing over there when I looked back and spotted three guys jump out of a van, pull Joe into the vehicle, and speed off. I ran after the minivan but couldn't stop them." I pointed. "They took off that way."

Raul squinted down the road. "You are from the States?"

"Yes, Austin."

"I have a cousin who lives in Austin. Beautiful city. My kids love to swim in Lake Travis. What can you tell me about the vehicle?"

"Gray minivan. Probably ten years old. Honda Odyssey, I think."

"Did it have plates?"

I thought about that for a moment. "No, I don't think so, actually. I don't recall seeing anything on the back."

"I'm not surprised," he said, jotting some notes on a small notepad. "What about these men? You say there were three of them?"

"Yes. All young guys. Probably early twenties. They were wearing regular T-shirts, jeans, and work boots. Two of them had facial hair. Goatees. The other guy was clean-shaven, I think."

"Any tattoos? Or other markings?"

I shook my head. "I don't know. It all happened really fast."

"Had you seen any of these men before today?"

"No, I don't think so."

"How many times have you been here to this village this week?"

"Three other times. We've been picking up groceries and other items for the orphanage. Has this kind of thing happened here before?"

Raul sighed. "Yes, I'm afraid so, Alex. Local criminals often look to exploit generous Americans like you who've crossed over our border to do God's work with the missions and orphanages here. They likely spotted you earlier this week and have been following you. They probably know you're over at Casa de Esperanza and were waiting for an opportunity. I'd expect a ransom note to arrive over there by morning."

"How would they go about delivering a ransom note?"

"They have their ways. Probably pay a kid to walk it over there."

"Is there anything the police can do?"

"I will interview the people here to see if anyone will talk, but it's unlikely. You see, these people are too afraid to speak up. But I will try my best. Then I'll go back to the station, enter this information into our system, and see if anything matches up. I promise we'll do everything we can. Maybe we'll get lucky."

"Do things like this usually turn out okay?"

"Depends. Do you have money?"

"Are you suggesting I pay the ransom?"

Raul took a moment, pressed his lips together. "I wish I could advise you otherwise and tell you not to pay. To allow us to find these men, bring them to justice, and get your father-in-law back safely. But this is a different world than in the States. We have the type of crime around here you likely never see in Austin. As police officers, we're doing everything we can to keep people safe. But we're overwhelmed right now. And I know the most important thing to you and your family is to have your loved one back with you as soon as possible. As much as I hate to admit it, the safest way to accomplish that without risking something happening to your father-in-law may be to pay."

"How much will they ask for?"

"Probably a couple thousand American dollars. It's a quick trick for them."

I nodded. "I appreciate you being straightforward about it."

This felt like an out-of-body experience. But I would gladly give them all our life savings to get Joe back safe and sound. The only reason Taylor and I even had extra money in the bank was because of my father-in-law. Three years ago, Joe had put $5 million into the software company I was starting, privately funding the whole venture. That investment had allowed me to hire the best team possible and be aggressive in the marketplace. Our company had taken off like a rocket and made all our personal dreams come true nearly overnight. We had just moved into an exquisite new house with a pool in an affluent neighborhood. The girls were in the best private schools. We'd taken them to Disney World three times in three years. We'd been able to support the charities we cared about with significant financial contributions. None of this would've been possible without Joe's unwavering support and belief in me.

"Do you have a photo of your father-in-law?" Raul asked.

I searched my phone, found one I'd taken just this morning of Joe holding Nicole in his arms, and texted it to the officer. I also spelled out Joe's full name. He told me to contact him if I remembered anything else that might be helpful; he'd reach out to me if he had any update.

"So what do I do now?" I asked him.

"Go back to your family, wait, and pray."

THREE

I drove slowly up the dirt road to Casa de Esperanza. I felt numb all over. I kept trying to figure out what I was going to say to Taylor when I got there, but the words just wouldn't form in my mind. There was no easy entry into a conversation about her father being kidnapped and held for ransom. But I did make the decision to tell her alone. Just the two of us. Give us a chance to process all this together first and then figure out how we would share it with my mother-in-law and the girls. Plus, if Taylor got really angry with me, I wanted her to be able to let me have it without Carol or the kids around. I deserved whatever Taylor wanted to spit at me right now.

Casa de Esperanza—House of Hope—sat on five acres of flat pastureland surrounded on all sides by a chain-link security fence. The main two-story building housed up to forty children. Most were elementary-age, but a few teenagers still lived at the facility. A second building next door contained the kitchen and eating space. There was also a small schoolhouse on the property with a couple of classrooms. That building was in the worst shape of all the structures. I thought it might collapse at any moment. I had been thinking about trying to raise money when I returned to Austin to help build the orphanage a brand-new schoolhouse. I couldn't imagine Olivia and Nicole getting their education in a building like that.

But then, I couldn't imagine a lot of things about life here for these kids. Most of them didn't even have decent shoes, so our first night we'd purchased dozens of boxes of new kids' shoes at a Payless shoe store in Brownsville and brought them to the orphanage with us the next day. These were cheap shoes, but the kids were beside themselves with joy as they tore open the boxes. It was like Christmas in July, with my daughters as the happy gift-giving elves.

I'd hoped this whole experience would leave a lasting impression on Olivia and Nicole and help them understand that most people did not live like we did back in Austin. Ours was a fantasy world. But I knew that fantasy would be completely shattered if we returned home without Joe.

I drove my Tahoe up to the gate of the property. The kids were all playing outside right now. Half of them were in the open field next to the main building, kicking soccer balls. I spotted my two girls on the steps in front of the main building, still dressed in princess outfits, along with a group of other girls. Olivia wore her favorite yellow Belle dress from *Beauty and the Beast*. She was a brunette like her mom, so she always liked to be a princess with the same hair color. Nicole was as blonde as can be, so she never wanted to dress up as any princess other than Elsa from *Frozen*. Carol was outside with them.

I got out of my vehicle and walked over to the chain-link gate, which was secured with a combination lock. My fingers were still shaking as I spun the dial back and forth. Because of this, it took me four tries before the lock released. I tugged the gate open, drove through the clearing, got back out, and locked everything up again. Then I parked my Tahoe in the short gravel drive right next to the orphanage's small yellow school bus. I sat there a moment, feeling my heart pounding in my chest. It was a surreal feeling being moments away from wrecking my wife with this news. Taking the deepest breath possible, I let it out slowly and said a little prayer. Then I opened the door and climbed out of my vehicle. I didn't even want to make eye contact with my mother-in-law. Had she already seen that I'd returned without Joe? I quickly glanced over to where Carol stood with the girls. Thankfully, she was too busy blowing bubbles in the air to pay much attention to me.

I headed straight for the building with the kitchen. I figured Taylor would be inside helping to get things ready for dinner. Even though I felt like a scared child, I knew I needed to be strong for my wife. I had to offer her some comfort and reassurance that everything was going to be okay. She could not see the fear I actually felt right now. I pulled open the door to the second building, stepped inside, and spotted Taylor in the large kitchen, working along with Esther and several other house moms. They were all busy sorting dishes and setting three long tables.

Taylor wore a light-blue hoodie, even though it was nearly 100 degrees Fahrenheit outside. My wife got cold at the slightest breeze. She glanced over at me standing by the door and gave me the same smile that had first slayed me when we were sixteen and back in high school together. We had both been involved in sports in those days. I excelled on the gridiron. She ran track. I flirted for a few months before finding the courage to ask her out. She said she'd only go out with me if I could beat her in a quarter-mile race—which was one full lap around the track. Ever cocky, I accepted the challenge. Our friends caught wind of it, and a dozen of them showed up after school. I barely stretched and kept cracking wise-ass jokes. But Taylor had on her "focus face," as I grew to call it, the whole time. Eyes narrow, brow bunched, lips pursed. One of Taylor's girlfriends sent us off at the starting line, and I quickly raced way out ahead. I kept glancing over my shoulder at her with an arrogant smile. But my legs started to feel rubbery around the final turn. She passed me thirty meters from the finish line while her girlfriends all whooped it up. I'll never forget the way she turned back to me and said, "Come on, slowpoke."

Fortunately, she agreed to go out with me anyway.

I loved her smile so much and wondered if this would be the last time it carried this much genuine joy. I couldn't smile back, no matter how hard I tried to force it. My lips just wouldn't move. Again, I felt the weight of the moment. She wiped her hands on a towel and walked over to me.

"Hey, where are the groceries?" she asked.

"I need to talk to you."

She tilted her head. "Okay."

"In private. Can we go out back?"

Her forehead bunched. "What's wrong?"

I could tell she already saw it on my face. I'd never been good at hiding anything from her. "Let's go outside."

Her eyes narrowed. "Just tell me, Alex. You're scaring me."

"Please, Taylor."

I reached out my hand for hers. She hesitantly placed her palm in mine. I walked her out the front of the building and circled around to the back, where we were alone and away from the chaos of the children playing. I turned to her, again tried to figure out where to start. But she beat me to it.

"Where's my dad?" she asked me.

I swallowed.

Her eyes widened. "What, Alex? What happened?"

"We were in the marketplace when some men jumped out of a van and grabbed your dad. I tried to stop them, but they pulled him into the van and drove away before I could do anything."

Taylor's whole body tightened. "What . . . ?"

"I spoke to the police. The officer told me this kind of thing has happened before around here, and everything usually turns out okay. They just want money. The police are going to do everything they can to find him."

My wife was not prone to outbursts of emotion. I was the one who cried while watching sappy movies. Taylor was more like her dad.

Steady. But I could see tears quickly forming in her eyes. I kept talking because I knew giving her as much information as possible would help her to hold things together.

"The officer I spoke with suspects these men may have spotted us in the village earlier this week. Maybe even followed us back here. They probably saw my nicer vehicle and put it together that we might be wealthy Americans. He thinks we'll likely get a ransom note at some point tonight. The officer called it a quick money trick."

"I can't believe this."

"I know. I'm so sorry, Taylor. I just didn't think—"

"What do I . . . How do I tell my mom?"

"We'll do it together. But I wanted to tell you first."

"Did they hurt him?"

I shook my head. "No, they just grabbed him and took off."

I left out the part about the black hood being pulled over his head. I thought that detail would only freak her out even more. I could see the wheels beginning to turn in my wife's mind. Taylor liked to be in control. She was immediately putting together a plan of action.

"We have to get to the bank," she said. "How much money will we need?"

"The officer says it's usually only a couple thousand dollars."

Taylor looked at her watch. "It's after five. The banks are already closed!"

"We'll get it first thing in the morning."

"What if it's too late by then?"

"It won't be."

"You don't know that, Alex!"

Tears were now falling down her cheeks. I pulled her in close to my chest, wrapped my arms tightly around her. Thankfully, she didn't resist.

"We'll get him back. I promise."

FOUR

My mother-in-law took the news about how I'd expected—an emotional explosion that left her gasping for air, clutching her chest, and nearly hyperventilating. For a moment, I wondered if we were going to have a second tragedy on our hands and have to rush her to the hospital. It took Taylor a minute to calm Carol down to the point where she could start to breathe again. The strength my wife showed in that moment with her mother overwhelmed me. But I'd seen this before. When Olivia was born, we nearly lost her that first night in the hospital. Everything had been fine, and then doctors were whisking our baby girl away for emergency heart surgery. I fell apart. But my wife was a rock. I'd never seen a woman pray like Taylor did throughout that night.

Together, the three of us decided we would wait to share anything with Olivia or Nicole about what had happened to Joe in the hope that we'd get him back by tomorrow, and everything would return to normal again. Raul had made it seem like that was a real possibility. Maybe we could spare my girls from the trauma. To her credit, Carol was able to gather herself enough to put on a good face while they began to eat dinner with all the kids and the staff at the orphanage. Esther told me they'd never experienced anything like a kidnapping situation. She was horrified and pledged to do whatever she could to help us.

Instead of eating dinner, I spent my time trying to be proactive in an effort to keep myself from having a nervous breakdown. I was on the phone with the US embassy in Mexico for more than an hour, trying to figure out if there was anything they could do. Unfortunately, their support seemed to be very limited. Still, they emailed me information on Mexican legal procedures, how to file a police report and seek prosecution, a list of Mexican attorneys, and a packet about emotional trauma support. I called one of the local attorneys on their list. He said he had a private investigator he trusted if I wanted to put down a significant retainer fee. It would have to be all cash. I told him I'd get him the money first thing in the morning.

When I couldn't take the waiting around anymore, I drove back over to the village to see if I'd missed anything. I stood in the exact spot where it all happened, but no new revelations came to me. I felt eyes on me and turned toward a building to my right. When I did, a man quickly slipped out of my view around a corner. But I'd caught enough of a glimpse to recognize it was the same clean-shaven guy in the gray suit I'd spotted in the crowd earlier. I walked over to the corner of the building and peered around it into a dirt alley. There was no sign of the guy anywhere. That was odd. Had he been watching me? Could the guy possibly be involved?

I called Raul. To this point, the police officer had been very responsive in keeping me updated with his progress over the past few hours. We'd spoken twice already. He told me that a new witness had given a vague description of the men and the van. But he was honest in saying it wasn't really much help. And unfortunately, nothing had turned up yet on the van. I mentioned the guy in the gray suit. Raul said he'd ask around about him. After getting into my Tahoe, I returned to the orphanage. No ransom note had arrived in my brief absence.

When it began to get late, Taylor and I decided it would be best for her and Carol to take the girls to our hotel. I would stay at the orphanage until this was all resolved and we got Joe back safe and sound. I prayed it would be just one night.

"What about Papa?" Olivia asked, climbing into the back seat of my Tahoe.

To this point, we had led our girls to believe Joe was still over at the village, meeting with local painters about assisting with our project.

Taylor helped get my daughter buckled. "I told you, baby. Papa and Daddy are going to stay at the orphanage tonight so they can get up *really* early tomorrow and begin working."

"Oh, yeah. Does that mean I get to sleep with Nanny tonight?"

"Sure, sweetie," Carol answered, sliding into the front passenger seat. "I would like that very much."

"Yay!" Olivia squealed. "And Nicky can sleep with Mommy."

"That's right," Taylor replied.

I glanced over and noticed that my five-year-old was already fast asleep in her car seat. The girls played so hard at the orphanage each day that they barely survived the car trip back to the hotel. Nicole was usually out within the first few minutes of the drive.

I leaned in and gave Olivia a kiss. "Be good for Mommy and Nanny, okay?"

"I will, I promise!" She gave me the biggest smile.

Her smile was a replica of her mom's and could light up an entire room. I wondered if my daughter's smile would also be permanently damaged should we not get Joe back soon. I walked around to where Taylor had climbed into the driver's seat. She had been silent for most of the evening. It was killing me. I craved some sense of normalcy from her. The numb feeling that had begun in me earlier had now spread to every part of my body. I felt desperate to break out of it.

"I'm going to do everything I can," I said, not even sure what that meant.

"Call me the minute you find out anything. No matter how late. I won't be sleeping anyway."

"I will. Taylor—"

"Just get him back, Alex. Please."

FIVE

I followed Esther around to the back of the kitchen building where the orphanage had guest quarters. She opened the door and led me inside. It was a simple room with a full-size bed, a dresser, a desk in the corner, and a small bathroom with a shower. Everything was nicely decorated with warm colors.

"There are brand-new toiletries in the bathroom," Esther mentioned. "If you need anything, please let me know."

"I appreciate it."

"And, Alex, we are all praying for Joe's safe return."

"Thank you, Esther."

She left me alone. I unzipped a brown backpack I'd had with me that had an extra T-shirt and blue jeans inside. I needed a shower badly. I had perspired hard all evening from both the extreme heat and my nerves. In the bathroom, I took the hottest shower possible to try to see if the beads of water could bring me any comfort. They didn't. I toweled off, got dressed in the T-shirt and jeans, and lay on the bed. I was emotionally exhausted but unsure how I could possibly sleep tonight with all this swirling through my head. As hard as I tried not to think about it, I kept wondering where Joe was and what he was doing. Did they have him in a dark room somewhere? Had they hurt him? Beat him?

Was Joe scared in spite of the unusually calm look on his face earlier? Again, I wondered how he could've appeared so steady. *I'm sorry.* Why had he said that?

I stared up at the ceiling of the bedroom. It was so quiet at the orphanage, which was pretty much in the middle of nowhere. Almost *too* quiet on a night like tonight. I could hear my own heart beating away in my eardrums. I closed my eyes but then opened them right back up when all I could see behind my eyelids was that black hood being yanked down over Joe's head. I took several deep breaths, tried to calm down again. But it was difficult. My father-in-law meant so much to me. Joe had been there for me through thick and thin, beginning on my worst day.

It had started to sprinkle, but that hadn't stopped me from continuing to shoot hoops in the cracked driveway of our modest middle-class home. I had no intention of going inside the house, where the better part of my extended family had all gathered. Aunts, uncles, cousins, my grandma, my older sister, and her husband—they were all in there. I checked my watch, did some quick math. My dad had now officially been dead for eight hours and twenty-two minutes. I kept calculating the time down to the very minute. I'm not sure why. It was just that surreal feeling of having him here one moment and then gone the next. I was only sixteen, and my father was never coming back.

I hadn't known my dad would die today when I'd woken up this morning. Sure, he'd been sick for the better part of six months. Leukemia sucked. I had watched it take my father's once-strong body and shrivel it up to near skin and bones. It had taken all his hair. But we'd thought he'd been doing better the past month. He seemed to be getting stronger. So it was a shock when my mom woke me up early, told me something was wrong and that she'd called for an ambulance. I had scrambled to throw on jeans and a T-shirt and hustled up the hallway to my parents' bedroom. My dad was lying on the bed and breathing heavily. His eyes were closed. I tried to stir him, to let him know I was there, but he didn't respond. At that point, I didn't know if he was even still with us, but I told him I loved him and to keep fighting, just in case he could hear me. My mom was in the kitchen, on the phone with her sister. I could hear the fear in her voice as she frantically explained what was happening.

The ambulance arrived a few minutes later, and medics hauled my father away. I only saw him one more time, at the hospital a few hours later, when a doctor told us it was time to say our goodbyes. I could barely register what all was happening while I stood in that hospital room with him lying motionless in that bed. And soon I was engulfed by family and neighbors, who had all rushed to the hospital. I'd barely had a moment to process any of this—not that I really wanted to anyway.

I took a shot with the basketball from the edge of the opened garage, but it came up way short. I didn't have much energy tonight. My head was spinning, and my body was in shock. I glanced over to a window of the house. Everyone had migrated from the hospital to our home, thinking we shouldn't be alone right now. That was probably true for my mom. But not for me. A few relatives had come out here to check on me but quickly got the hint and left me to myself. I checked my watch again. Eight hours and twenty-nine minutes. I spotted another pair of headlights, and then a nice black Mercedes sedan parked along the curb in front of our three-bedroom house. A trim man with thick brown-grayish hair got out. He wore khakis, a blue sweater, and black dress shoes. Taylor's father.

I was surprised to see him. I had been dating his daughter for only a couple of months. After Taylor had spent the day with me at the hospital, I told her to go on home—I just needed alone time. So it was curious to see her father now walking up the driveway toward me. We were really just getting to know each other. I had found him to be a pleasant man with a gentle spirit. He wasn't one of those stereotypical intimidating fathers who had threatened to end my life if I ever hurt his little girl. I'd liked him from the beginning.

I tucked the basketball under my arm. "Mr. Dobson."

"Mind if I join you, Alex?"

I tilted my head. "Shooting hoops?"

"Sure. I think I've still got some game left."

I shrugged. "All right."

I passed him the ball. He dribbled once to his left and fired up a shot from about fifteen feet out. It swished. I smiled, retrieved the ball, passed it back out to him. He tossed up another and made it.

"I didn't realize you played basketball, Mr. Dobson."

"Starting point guard in high school."

"Really? Cool."

"Hey, I'd like you to start calling me Joe, okay?"

"Oh, okay."

We passed the ball around, took some more shots. It felt good to just be doing something normal with someone. And unlike the others, Joe wasn't treating me like a porcelain doll that might break if he suddenly said the wrong thing. That's not what I needed right now. The rain started to come down heavier, so we took a break and huddled inside the covering of the garage.

"You going to be on the basketball team again this year?" Joe asked.

"I think so. Although my football coach would rather me spend the off-season focusing on my footwork and throwing hundreds of balls a day. So we'll see."

I was the starting quarterback on varsity and getting some good looks by college recruiters. My future was probably in football.

"I think it's good for you to play a lot of sports at your age."

"That's what my dad always says . . ." I paused, swallowed. "Or said."

I felt the sudden weight of that phrase, cursed, then was embarrassed.

"Sorry, Mr. Dob . . . I mean, Joe."

"No need to apologize, Alex. I think a bit of cursing is appropriate on a day like today." He gave me a tight smile. "You know, I lost my father in a car crash when I was young. Not quite as young as you, but it was still a

shock. It took me a long time to speak of him in the past tense. That made it real."

"It doesn't seem real right now."

"It may not for a long time. You don't need to rush it."

I nodded. I liked talking to Joe. He just had a steady way about him that made conversation easy. I'd been nervous as hell when I'd first met him a couple of months ago. Taylor spoke of her dad like he hung the moon. He was her hero in every way. So I felt insecure going into that first dinner at her house. Plus, her family had loads of money. Mine did not. Taylor lived in a huge house with a pool in a rich neighborhood. We lived in this run-down tract home on a street lined with nearly identical houses. My father was a construction contractor who made just enough to pay the mortgage and keep food on the table. Joe was a successful attorney. But he had never made me feel uncomfortable about it or implied that I wasn't good enough for his only daughter.

"Your mother is going to really need you to step up," Joe said to me.

"I know. It's just us now. We're alone."

He put his hand on my shoulder. "You're not alone, okay?"

I shrugged. "Yeah, I mean, I got family in there, I guess."

"I don't mean them, Alex. I mean me."

I tilted my head, surprised to hear him say that.

Joe continued. "I want you to know I'm here for you, son, regardless of what becomes of your relationship with my daughter. I want you to feel free to call me, day or night, with whatever is on your mind. I know this won't be an easy road for you. A young man losing a father is devastating. But I've been there, and I want to be here for you. If you're okay with that."

I met his eyes. I could tell he meant it. I was startled by the sudden swell of emotions that began to bubble up inside of me. I didn't know what to say, so I just nodded. But I also couldn't fight off the tears that were starting to form in my eyes. I tried to stop myself. The last thing I wanted was to cry in front of Taylor's dad. But I couldn't help myself. Especially when I saw Joe's eyes suddenly grow wet. That's when the damn burst. So I let go and allowed every emotion I'd buried inside me to pour out. Joe put his hand on my shoulder, pulled me in closer, and held me like I was his own son.

I heard a dinging noise come from my backpack. A phone message alert. But it wasn't my phone, which was sitting on the bed right next to me. Getting up, I fetched my backpack, unzipped a front pocket, and pulled out Joe's cell phone. I had shoved it in there earlier after returning from the village. While the phone was locked with security, I knew the password because Joe had dozens of children's apps and movies on it for my girls to enjoy whenever we were out to dinner together—which was at least twice a week. I typed in the password and found a dozen or so new messages waiting to be addressed. Most looked like normal business emails. Joe had been an attorney his entire professional career. Although he called himself retired now, Joe still represented a few cases here and there from his home office. Out of curiosity, I did a quick scan and noted that most of the messages were indeed related to various legal matters. But the latest alert that had just arrived was a text message from a number not in Joe's contacts.

Call me ASAP. I think we've been found out.

Greta

My eyes narrowed on the message. There was no text history between them that suggested they'd previously exchanged messages. *I think we've been found out.* What did that mean? My thoughts were interrupted when my own phone rang on the bed next to me. Taylor. I leaned over and grabbed it.

"Hey," I answered.

"Anything?" she asked.

"No. Still nothing."

She sighed. "This is excruciating."

"I know."

"Olivia wants to say good night," Taylor said.

My seven-year-old jumped on the phone. "Hi, Daddy!"

"Hi, baby girl. Are you about to go to Nanny's room?"

"Yes!"

"Don't be too much of a wiggle worm, okay? Nanny needs to get a good night's sleep tonight."

"I won't. Good night, Daddy. I love you."

"I love you, too, sweetie. Good night."

Taylor was back on the phone. "Nicole is out like a light. There's no stirring her without getting the monster in return."

The monster was what we called Nicole when her sleep was interrupted before she was ready to get up. She had a deep growl for a tiny girl. It was no fun dealing with the monster.

"She went nonstop all day long," I said.

"Yeah. I'll bathe her in the morning."

A lull of silence. I could hear Taylor nervously breathing.

"Try to get some sleep, babe," I said.

"My mind keeps going to the worst possible places."

"I know." I tried to think of something comforting to say but felt lost for words. So I simply said, "I love you."

"I love you, too."

I hung up and felt my eyes grow moist.

SIX

I left my guest quarters and walked the orphanage property to see if someone had dropped off a ransom note somewhere. How would they even leave a note? Would someone tape it to a door? I had no idea. I first checked the front doors of each of the buildings and then the exterior of the security gate before I settled into a weathered rocking chair tucked in the night shadows near the front of the main building and watched the dirt road. There was no reason to stay in my bedroom. I wouldn't be sleeping anyway. I perked up a few times when I spotted headlights approaching. But each time the car would pass by the orphanage without slowing down.

Taylor was also up all night. She texted me at midnight, at two-thirty, and at four in the morning. I always texted right back, telling her I had no update. It was grueling. I wanted to offer my wife hope. But I was losing hope by the hour. Just as the sun was popping up on a new day, I spotted the familiar police truck from yesterday drive down the isolated dirt road and pull up to the security gate. Raul got out. I had texted him the previous night to let him know I was staying at the orphanage overnight should anything come up on his end. Why was he here now? He had my phone number. If he had news, he could have just called.

I felt a surge of anxiety push through me. I hurried down the gravel drive to meet him outside the gate. The lines in his face told me he was not here to deliver a positive update. We exchanged a very quick greeting.

"I need you to come with me, Alex," he said.

"Why?"

Raul pressed his lips firmly together. "We got a call about an explosion this morning. When we arrived at the scene a few minutes ago, we discovered a vehicle on fire matching the description you gave me yesterday."

"A gray minivan?"

"Yes. And there's a body inside."

That news hit me like a full punch to the chest. "Is it Joe?"

"We don't know yet. I need to see if you can make an ID."

I rode with him in silence, feeling a desperation I'd experienced only once in my life—at Olivia's birth—settling on me. That nauseated feeling of being caught in the middle of extreme opposite emotions. I was about to experience total devastation or unbridled relief. There was no room for anything in between. As we passed by a rickety old shack, I spotted an older couple standing outside. Raul told me the call about the explosion came from the woman, who said it had startled her and her husband awake. We pulled off the desolate road. From the passenger seat, I could see two police vehicles on the scene, along with an ambulance and a fire truck. The minivan was no longer on fire, but it was still heavily smoking. Several firefighters were examining the wreckage. Although completely burned, the vehicle definitely looked like the same kind of minivan the three men had used yesterday to grab Joe.

After getting out, I followed Raul around the other vehicles. On the opposite side of the burned vehicle, I noticed a medic zipping up a black body bag. The sight of it stole my breath. Someone was clearly dead. But was it Joe? I kept praying this was all somehow a bad coincidence.

That this was a different minivan, and whoever was in that body bag was not my father-in-law.

A young officer walked over to Raul, glanced at me, and then the two officers had a conversation in Spanish I couldn't understand. My eyes drifted back over to the vehicle, searching desperately for anything that might not match up with what I saw yesterday. But it was too hard to tell. Nothing was left of the minivan except the metal frame. The younger officer gave Raul a small black bag and walked away.

Raul turned to face me. "The body is burned badly, Alex, especially in the upper region around the shoulders, neck, and head. I don't mean to be overly graphic, but we won't be able to determine anything by facial recognition. But it is a male about five-foot-ten with a slender build. Does that match up with your father-in-law?"

I swallowed, nodded.

"Two items were recovered," Raul said. "A small belt buckle and a ring."

Raul started to open the bag. I thought about how Joe always wore a black golf belt with a little silver buckle with the Titleist logo on it. Was he wearing it today? I couldn't remember, but my heart was pounding so fast.

Raul gently poured the contents of the bag into the palm of his left hand. A charred belt buckle and a ring. I immediately recognized the word *Titleist* on the buckle. And it looked like Joe's gold wedding ring. Still, I didn't want to believe it. This couldn't be happening. I reached down with a shaky hand, picked up the ring, and looked inside to see if there was an inscription.

I felt my heart collapse.

Joe and Carol. Always, Forever.

SEVEN

I could barely focus on the highway as I drove across the border and made my way back to the Holiday Inn. Taylor had already called and texted me three times since I'd been at the scene of the explosion. I hadn't responded yet. I had to get to her as fast as possible. There was no way I was going to tell her what had just happened over the phone. Twice I had to pull over on the side of the highway to try to catch my breath and calm down. But it barely worked. The closer I got to the hotel, the faster my heart raced. I worried I might have a full-on panic attack. But I had to hold it together for Taylor.

I pulled into the parking lot and settled in a spot close to the front doors of the hotel. I sat there a moment, knowing I couldn't go inside and do this in front of the kids. I typed out a text to Taylor, paused before sending it.

I'm in the hotel parking lot. Please come down alone.

I took a deep breath and then let it out as slowly as possible. I knew sending this text would initiate one of the most brutal moments of our lives. The tipping of a domino that would change everything in devastating ways. I needed to be ready. It was time for me to show Taylor the same kind of strength she'd demonstrated to me over the years.

I sent the text. Taylor bolted out the front doors of the hotel two minutes later. She scanned the parking lot until she spotted our Tahoe. I could see the fear pouring out of her eyes. Of course, she knew something was wrong. There would've been no other explanation as to why I hadn't called or texted her back until now. It crushed me to have to confirm that fear in her.

I got out of the Tahoe and walked around to the front of the vehicle. She ran over to me and then slowed a few feet away, as if she were trying to read my face before I ever said anything. But I could see she already knew.

"No! Don't you say it!"

I stepped toward her. "I'm so sorry, Taylor."

"No, Alex! No!"

I grabbed her arms with both hands, pulled her all the way into me, even though she was trying to yank away. She kept screaming, "No! No!" and fought me for several seconds. But I didn't let go. Finally, she buried her face into my chest. The full weight of her suddenly collapsed in my arms, as if she had nothing left, and all I could do was keep her from dropping to the pavement.

EIGHT

It took us a couple of days of coordinating with Raul and the police, the US consulate in Matamoros because it was an international death, and a local funeral home, where we had Joe's body cremated—or what was left of it—before we finally packed everything up in the Tahoe and drove back to Austin.

I had originally wanted Taylor to take her mother and the kids home without me on that first day and let me handle everything, but she thought it would be even more traumatic for our girls to immediately yank them out of the trip. I had to admit she was right. The remaining time with the other orphanage kids helped to ease some of the initial shock and grief our girls had felt when we told them the tragic news about Papa's death in a car accident. We decided to not go into the horrific details of what really happened at this point. There were a lot of gut-wrenching tears with my girls that first day and plenty of discussions of heaven. Taylor somehow put aside her own shattered heart to make sure the girls processed their hurt first. On the other hand, Carol simply shut down on us when she received the news about her husband. There was no emotional outburst from her the second time around. My mother-in-law just went white-faced and stoic. It was an awful thing to witness, as if watching the blood drain completely out of her body within a matter of seconds. Carol had remained rather emotionless the past two days. Even my girls couldn't seem to get her to smile.

By the time we left Brownsville, Raul still had no real answers for me as to what had happened to Joe and why we'd never had the chance to pay a ransom. None of it made any sense to him or to his colleagues unless it truly was a tragic accident—a kidnapping effort gone horribly wrong. But Raul promised me he would continue to investigate and keep me updated with their progress. Then he gave me a homemade card his kids had made for my family to try to comfort us in our loss. It was a nice gesture.

We made the five-hour drive home in near silence—other than the sound of *Beauty and the Beast* playing on repeat on the drop-down TV for the girls. I kept looking over to Taylor, wanting to say something comforting, but I had no words. I was as numb as she was. None of this felt real. Two days ago, Joe had been sitting in the same passenger seat next to me. Now he was gone. I kept expecting to somehow snap out of this nightmare and find us all together again—like the trip had never happened. My mind was a mosh pit of shock, guilt, and sadness, and I could hardly put any thoughts together. It didn't help that I hadn't slept much at all the past two nights.

How would we all get through this?

Where did we even go from here as a family?

I finally pulled my Tahoe into our three-car garage around nine that evening and parked next to Taylor's Lexus SUV. We had insisted that Carol stay with us for at least the first week back in Austin. While Taylor and my mother-in-law carried our sleepy girls inside the house, I unloaded all the luggage, including the ceramic white container with Joe's ashes that I'd purchased at the funeral home. I wasn't sure what to do with it, so I went into my home office and put it on my desk.

For a second, I just stared at the container. I kept reliving that moment in the village. I'd briefly hesitated when those men had grabbed Joe. If only I'd reacted more quickly, maybe I could have gotten to the minivan before they'd shut that door. Maybe I could have somehow stopped all this. But I did hesitate. And now I'd have to live with that harsh reality for the rest of my life.

I heard the pitter-patter of little feet running around upstairs. Olivia and Nicole had gotten fresh wind. They were probably excited to be back home with all their dolls and toys again. It would likely take us an hour to get them settled back down. That might've annoyed me prior to the trip, but I welcomed it right now. I needed to hear my girls having fun. I needed to feel that full life from them. In this moment, it was salve for a wound so deep, I doubted it would ever heal. I knew our girls' laughter might be the only chance we all had at making it through this brutal next week.

When we finally did get Olivia and Nicole tucked into bed, they were both out within seconds. Although our new house had five bedrooms, the girls still wanted to share a room. So we put them in the biggest. Taylor and Carol had decorated their bedroom like it was a Disney exhibit. Both girls had their own princess beds with pink-and-purple canopies hanging from the ceiling filled with tiny white twinkle lights. Built-in white shelves went floor to ceiling on one side of the room and were crammed with more stuffed animals and dolls than I could count. A local artist had painted a full mural on the other side of the room that showed all the Disney princesses dancing along with our girls at a ball together. It was a little girl's dream bedroom. I felt fortunate they could sleep in such a magical place on a night like tonight. Maybe it would protect them from nightmares about Papa no longer being with us.

I kissed them both on the forehead, left the bedroom, and went downstairs. The door to the guest bedroom was cracked open, so I took a quick peek inside to check on my mother-in-law. She had not yet changed into her sleepwear. She was still wearing her travel clothes and was just sitting in a cushioned chair in the corner, looking blankly out the window toward the front circular driveway. Her luggage was untouched on the bed where I'd left it earlier. I gently knocked on the bedroom door. Carol looked over at me.

"Do you need anything?" I asked.

She shook her head. "Just need to sit here for a quiet moment and gather my thoughts."

"I understand."

"Thank you for everything the past two days, Alex. I could not have managed any of this on my own."

"I don't want you to worry, Carol. I'll take care of everything."

"I know you will. Because you're just like Joe."

I swallowed. "Try to get some rest."

"I will. Good night."

It broke my heart to see Carol this way. I wanted to somehow lift her spirits and thought about Lizzie, her Yorkshire terrier. A neighborhood kid had been taking care of her dog all week at my in-laws' house two blocks over. We'd originally discussed not getting Lizzie until the morning. However, seeing Carol so distraught made me want to change that plan. She loved that dog. So did my kids. They would all probably enjoy having her in our home when they woke up the next day.

I headed back to my bedroom to run it past Taylor, but she was already in bed with the lights out. I knew she was exhausted. So I crossed through the house, laced up my running shoes in the back hallway, opened a garage door, and took a late-night stroll in our neighborhood. Rollingwood, where we lived, was an affluent community of expensive homes set in a lush landscape just a couple of miles west of downtown proper. Our move into this neighborhood had made my commute to the office a quick ten minutes and allowed me to go back and forth from work during the day if there was something I wanted to do with the girls. That was a huge blessing because the drive to our previous home in South Austin had taken me thirty minutes each way. Living in this neighborhood gave our family easy access to the trails and parks around Lady Bird Lake—the beautiful stretch of the

Colorado River that weaves through the heart of the city. Since we'd moved in six months ago, Taylor and I had been able to take our girls to several Broadway shows and concerts, and we were now regulars at various sporting events involving our alma mater, the University of Texas. The girls loved to dress up in their Longhorns cheerleader outfits every chance they could get.

Life had been so good for us here. Would it all change now that Joe was gone? We had been cruising down a road of ease and comfort, but now it felt like we'd swerved off and were tumbling down the side of a mountain.

I walked two blocks up a small hill, passing by my neighbors, most of whose lights were already off, and then stepped up to my in-laws' one-story ranch-style house. The home sat on a spacious corner lot and had an incredible view of the downtown skyline from the back patio. Joe had purchased the home right after Taylor had graduated from college because he wanted everything on one level instead of the two-story house nearby where Taylor had grown up. I wondered if Carol would be able to afford to keep the house. I'd start figuring that out tomorrow. So much about the future was now up in the air. It all felt so sudden. Even when I'd lost my own father, I'd had some time in advance to think about the possibility.

I followed the driveway up to their garage and found the security keypad on the outside wall. Punching in the code, I watched the first garage door ease up into the ceiling. Joe's shiny gray Mercedes sedan sat in the garage next to Carol's Range Rover. For a moment, I just stared at Joe's car. I'd watched him get in and out of that vehicle so many times over the past couple of years. There were car seats in the back for my girls. My in-laws took them everywhere. I again felt struck by the stark reality that Joe would never sit behind that steering wheel again. He'd never again open the back door for my kids to jump inside. He'd never give me that two-finger salute he always did before driving away with them—his way of saying, "I'll take care of your girls for you."

Sighing, I eased around the vehicle and made my way to the door to the house. Opening it, I was surprised that I didn't hear the alarm beep go off, letting me know the house was currently secured. Had the neighborhood kid not been setting the alarm each night after feeding Lizzie and letting her out? Although I did not hear the alarm beep, I did hear Lizzie as clear as day. She was barking up a storm from somewhere inside the house. Did she hear me open the garage? Was that why she was barking? If so, why wasn't she racing around the corner to the back hallway, where I now stood? My in-laws usually let Lizzie have free rein of the house, even when they weren't home. Did they ask their dog sitter to keep her locked inside a room? The barking surprised me. Lizzie was not usually a barker, even when random people came to the front door.

I flipped on a light switch in the back hallway, made my way into the kitchen. The barking grew louder. It sounded like Lizzie was locked in a room down the long hallway to the bedrooms. I turned on the kitchen lights, walked across the living room toward the bedroom hallway.

"Lizzie!" I called out. "Calm down. It's me."

But she just kept at it. For how long had she been doing this? I opened the door to the first bedroom. Lizzie bolted right out and didn't even pause for a moment to acknowledge me. She would usually try to lick me silly. Instead, she raced around the corner of the dark hallway, back toward the master bedroom. Now she was both growling and barking. What the hell?

"Lizzie, what are you doing?"

I hurried after her, turned the corner, then froze in place. I stood face-to-face with a man dressed in all black. I recognized him immediately. He was the same Mexican guy in the gray suit I'd spotted in the village crowd when Joe had been abducted. The same guy who had been watching me from a distance later that night before disappearing in the dirt alley. What was he doing here?

Before I could react, he charged at me, kicking at my legs and throwing a punch toward my face. I was able to block the punch with my wrist but couldn't keep from tripping over his leg kick. I fell hard, straight onto my back on the hardwood. My head collided with the floor, and I completely lost my breath. The intruder did not stick around to further assault me. He jumped over me and ran around the corner. Lizzie took off after him, barking the entire way. I tried to push myself up but fell back again because I was dizzy. I heard a back patio door open and quickly shut.

I carefully pushed myself up again, got to my feet, and then kind of stumbled through the living room to the back door, where Lizzie was still yapping away. Staring into the backyard, I couldn't see anyone in the glow of the landscape lighting. The guy was probably already long gone. Lizzie stopped barking but was still pacing and huffing in a tight circle by the back door. I reached down, scooped her up, and began petting her.

"It's okay, girl. Everything's okay."

But my heart was racing. I pulled out my phone, dialed 911, told the dispatcher what had just happened. Then I hung up and waited for the police to arrive. I again stared into the darkness of the backyard. The whole thing had me rattled. I couldn't believe the same guy from the village had been inside my in-laws' house. Why? Was he robbing the place? If the guy was somehow involved with Joe's kidnapping, he certainly could've had my father-in-law's home address. Joe's wallet was never recovered. But would he really travel all this way to rob a house? I did a quick search of the rooms. Nothing seemed out of place. I even found some of my mother-in-law's expensive jewelry sitting out in the open in a jewelry box on top of her vanity. The guy hadn't touched it.

So why had he really been here tonight?

NINE

I dealt with two police officers for the next thirty minutes. I gave them a full report of what had happened, a description of the guy, and then told them I was certain I'd recognized him from our trip to Mexico. As far as I could tell, nothing had been stolen unless the guy had put something inside his pants pockets before our encounter. Two security cameras were on the property—one by the front door, and the other by the garage—but I didn't have access to the phone security app to review the footage. I told the officers I would do that as soon as I got back home and was able to look on my father-in-law's phone. I would call and let them know if anything turned up. The officers did one more sweep of the property and finally left.

I packed up a small bag with Lizzie's essentials, put her on a leash, and then returned home with her. The guest bedroom was now dark, so I didn't bother letting Carol know I had Lizzie with me. Hopefully, the dog would put a small smile on her face first thing in the morning. I left Lizzie in the laundry room, where we had a dog bed for her, and made sure she had fresh bowls of food and water. I then quietly returned to the master bedroom, where Taylor was still tucked under the covers with the lights out, and found my way to the back of our closet. Shutting the door to the closet, I turned on the light and spotted my backpack in the corner.

Sitting on a stool, I unzipped the front pocket and grabbed Joe's cell phone from inside. I wanted to check the security app on his phone to see if either of the cameras at his house had caught a glimpse of the intruder. Powering up the phone, I began to see new message notifications appear on the screen. Ignoring them, I searched for the security app and opened it. I knew how to work the app because we had the same security system monitoring our house. I reviewed security footage from the past couple of hours but couldn't find any sign of the intruder. The guy must've entered from the same place he'd exited—the back patio. No camera there. I again wondered about the house alarm. Why was it not armed? I would check tomorrow with the teenage dog sitter.

At the moment, I didn't plan on telling Carol or Taylor about the break-in, especially when it didn't look like anything had been stolen. They were both emotionally fragile right now—especially my mother-in-law. I didn't want to send her over the edge. Not yet, at least. Still, I felt unsettled. Was Joe possibly targeted for a reason beyond being recognized as a wealthy American? I went back to the main screen on Joe's phone and began scrolling through the various messages that had arrived since I'd pulled it out the other night. Not for any reason other than it gave me a brief escape from reality. The people who had tried to communicate with my father-in-law over the past two days had no idea he was dead. Other than family and close friends, we hadn't yet gone to the effort to let the rest of the world know the tragic news. I envied these people. I also wanted to live in a world where Joe was still alive.

I paused on one of the unread text messages. It came from the same Greta who had sent Joe the unusual message the other night.

What is going on? Call me!

My eyes narrowed. The text message felt completely out of place among the other business-related messages. It seemed personal. I thought about the previous one. *I think we've been found out.* Found out? By whom? What did that mean? I didn't recognize the area code, so I did a quick Google search and discovered it was a DC phone number. That gave me another pause. DC? Joe had just flown up to DC for a legal conference a few days before our Mexico trip. For a fleeting moment, a disturbing thought popped into my mind. An affair? I shook my head, quickly dismissed it. I couldn't imagine my father-in-law doing something like that or keeping that kind of secret.

Still, the two texts from her were odd. Could they possibly be related to what had just happened to Joe? I called the phone number on Joe's phone. Maybe I could put my anxieties to rest. It was nearly eleven here, which meant it would be midnight there. But this person seemed to want to talk to Joe right away. Plus, I was planning on reaching out to all his friends and associates starting tomorrow anyway.

The phone rang three times before a woman quietly answered.

"Thank God you're okay. I've been so worried."

For a second, I didn't know what to say. Worried?

"Joe?" she queried in a hushed tone.

I finally responded. "Is this Greta?"

She paused, then: "Who is this?"

"My name is Alex Mahan. I'm Joe's son-in-law."

Another long pause. "Why are you calling me from Joe's phone?"

"I'm sad to say Joe passed away two days ago."

She didn't respond like I'd expected. No audible gasp. No words of shock.

"What happened?" she simply asked.

"Joe was abducted while we were on a family trip to Mexico. He died in a car fire. Police think it was an accident in a ransom situation gone wrong."

Again, no shock or dismay. Just silence. Who was this woman?

"How did you know Joe?" I asked her.

The phone line suddenly went dead. I stared at the screen and saw that the call had ended. What the hell? Did she just hang up on me? I called the number back. It went straight to an automated voice mail. I didn't leave a message. Maybe hanging up was her way of absorbing the shock of it all. Still, if calling her was supposed to have helped alleviate any initial suspicious thoughts, it hadn't worked. But the truth was—in the highly unlikely event that Joe might have been having an affair with someone—I didn't want to know anything about it. Joe was gone. I had no desire to uncover dirt on him now. And I certainly didn't want a suspicion like that ever getting back to Carol or Taylor.

After brushing my teeth, I climbed into bed. Taylor was awake. I found her under the covers with tears running down her face. I had wondered when she'd finally break.

"Do you want to talk?" I whispered.

She shook her head. "Just hold me."

I wrapped my arms around her. She leaned fully into me, rested her head on my chest, and continued to cry. These were not deep sobs. Just a steady release of emotions I knew she'd kept buried inside the past two days in order to be strong for her mother and for our girls. Because she would step out of our bedroom each morning and try to be a superhero for our family, I needed to make sure I gave her a safe space to process her heartache. But I felt helpless. I wanted to fix this pain for Taylor so badly but couldn't do a damn thing. This woman was my everything. And to think I almost stupidly let her walk away eleven years ago. If not for Joe.

The fight had started at her college apartment. It had been my fault. Taylor had caught me in a lie. I'd brushed off dinner with her family the previous night and had told her I'd had a mandatory football team study-hall session. The truth was, I simply wanted to go out drinking with some of the other guys on the team and didn't want to get any pushback from her about it. One of her girlfriends busted me. It was the second time Taylor had caught me in the same kind of lie this past month. She was furious. I'd been able to wiggle my way out of the first situation, but she wasn't having it the second time around. She went off on me, said she could no longer trust me. And because trust was everything in a relationship, that meant we were done.

Then she stormed off, got in her car, and sped away.

I didn't go after her. After five years together, I wasn't so sure about us anymore. Taylor was all I'd ever known. And because I was on the football team at a place like the University of Texas, I had pretty girls constantly showering me with undeserved attention. I also felt pressure from some of my teammates to live it up while I still had the chance. I had not yet given in to that temptation. But I was flirting dangerously close to it. I felt confused. I certainly didn't want to hurt Taylor. But I also didn't want to lie to her anymore. I was at a crossroads, uncertain of the right path forward.

When I needed to find clarity about something, I would often go to a driving range near campus and hit golf balls. That's where Joe found me that night. I was all by myself at the very end of the range and had already made my way through half a bucket of balls. Only a couple of other golfers were out here with me tonight. I really wasn't much of a golfer yet. But I liked the game and was trying to get better. Taylor's dad had introduced me to the sport back in high school. Joe was an excellent golfer.

I spotted him walking toward me up the range wearing khaki shorts, a blue polo shirt, and brown loafers with no socks. I just kept on swinging my club and knocking balls as far as I could at various targets in the wide-open field of green. I knew why he was here. Taylor had probably gone straight to her parents' house, told them what had happened—how I was a lying jackass and all—and now her father was here to rip me a new one for the way I'd treated his daughter. That was fine. I deserved whatever harsh words Joe had for me, but I wasn't going to stop what I was doing and beg for it. He settled about fifteen feet from me, crossed his arms, and didn't say anything for a moment. I took another swing with my driver and watched the ball sail off into the distance.

"I think you're getting ahead of the ball," Joe said. "That's probably why you're not getting through your swing with as much power as you want. Make sure you keep your head steady, and stay behind the ball."

I put another golf ball on the tee, took my stance, pulled the driver all the way back, focused on what he'd just said, and then swung the club. The ball rocketed forward straight as an arrow and landed about thirty yards farther than my previous drive. I hid a smile. Joe always had a way of doing that. A few solid words of advice, and everything just seemed right.

"Yeah, that's it," Joe said. "Let's see you do it again."

I teed up another and took a big swing. I again connected beautifully and sent this ball even farther than the last.

"That's a perfect release," Joe mentioned. "Sometimes small things can make a big difference. Golf is a lot like life in that way."

I grabbed my six-iron from my golf bag and began hitting shorter shots. Joe made suggestions here and there to improve my swing, and each time I hit the ball better. We did this for the next twenty minutes as I worked my way through the clubs in my bag. Not once did he bring up anything about Taylor. I appreciated that. When I started to work up a good sweat, Joe went over to the small clubhouse and grabbed us a couple of bottles of cold water.

It dawned on me that if Taylor and I didn't make it, I would likely lose moments like this with her father. That really bummed me out. The man had walked step-by-step with me these past five years. He'd helped me get through my own father's death. He'd traveled with me across the country when I'd gone on several college football recruiting trips and had helped guide me to the decision to stay in Austin and play ball at UT. He'd gotten me through the pain of a knee injury a year ago that put me on the bench and had basically spoiled any chance I'd had at pursuing football profession-ally. He'd given me academic advice when I was struggling to find a specific degree plan to pursue. In every way, Joe had stepped into my life as a second father to me. I would be losing a lot more than just Taylor.

I looked over at him. "Guess we won't be playing golf together anymore, huh?"

"Well, that's up to you, Alex. I said from the very beginning, our friendship wasn't conditional."

"Yeah, well, Taylor might have different thoughts."

He chuckled. "I can't deny that."

"Look, Joe, I know I shouldn't have lied to her."

"Yeah, lying is never good," he agreed.

"Especially with Taylor. It's the most important thing."

Joe sighed. "I taught her from birth that honesty in a relationship is a gift to be protected. It's like a beautiful snow-capped mountain. Lies are the small cracks in the ice layer beneath the snow. They can seem innocent at first. We can even rationalize them as honorable. But once they start, it's hard as hell to stop them—until everything suddenly fractures. Then you have a full-on avalanche on your hands that could crush you. Believe me, I know."

"You do?"

He gave me a tight smile. "A story for another day."

"Well, between us, I don't know what I want right now. I'm feeling overwhelmed."

"That's understandable. You're at a critical moment in your life. You'll both be graduating soon and having to step out into the real world. It's smart to really think things through and figure out where you want to go in life. And who you might want beside you on that journey."

"Taylor seems to already know. At least, she did before tonight."

"My daughter likes to make a plan and then stick with it. We're the same in that way. Which means we don't do well with unexpected curveballs. But that doesn't mean our plans are always the right plans."

"Yeah, she's pretty stubborn."

"She gets that from me. Sorry."

I gave him a small smile. "I don't want to hurt Taylor."

"I know. But she's a big girl. She'll be okay. So will you. Believe me, life does move on, and hearts do heal over time. Whether together or apart, you both have incredibly bright futures ahead of you."

I took a drink of water, looked out over the range. "What do you think I should do?"

"Guess that depends. Do you still love her?"

I answered without hesitation. "Yes."

He pressed his lips together, took a long moment to respond, as if he'd been trying to get a gauge on me tonight. "You know, Alex, I had this putter back in college. It was the same putter my dad had given me when I was ten and first started playing golf with him. I loved that putter. I was so comfortable with it in my hands. I knew exactly how it should feel, the proper way to pull it back and then follow through with my stroke, even the precise sound it was supposed to make when I made perfect contact with the ball. I trusted that putter so much. When my other clubs failed me, I could always count on it. And because of that, I won a lot of youth golf tournaments. But then one day, on a whim, I went out and got myself a brand-new putter."

"Why?"

"Well, my friends were all getting brand-new gear. Golf was becoming more popular, and all these fancy new clubs and putters were being offered. They looked cool and were supposed to have all this new technology built into them. I got caught up in all that excitement, so I did what all my buddies were doing and purchased a new set of clubs. The first tournament I entered was a complete disaster. I hit my new irons okay, but I never missed so many putts in my entire life. I just couldn't get comfortable with it. Because of that, I finished near the bottom of the leaderboard. When it was over, I realized I'd made a big mistake."

"So you switched back to your old putter?"

"It was too late. I'd already donated my old set to a golf charity. When I went to look for my putter, they'd given it away with no record of who took it. So I had to live with that mistake."

"Dang, Joe. That must've sucked."

"*Yep, and I always regretted it. My golf game was never quite the same.*"

I could see where Joe was going with this story, although I doubted Taylor would appreciate being compared to a golf putter. Was I really willing to risk my whole future to satisfy some momentary curiosity?

"*What if it's too late for me, too?*" *I asked him.*

He grinned. "Something tells me it's not too late. But you've got a hell of a lot of work to do to make this right."

Joe had saved me that night.

But I couldn't return the favor days ago. Tears now hit my eyes.

I held my wife close to me and cried along with her.

TEN

I had a difficult night of sleep, in spite of my own exhaustion. I kept reliving my physical altercation with the mystery guy inside my in-laws' house. He had certainly been quick with his hands and feet, as if he knew certain martial arts, which made me ponder even more who he was. I had texted Raul about the encounter late last night and received a return text from him first thing this morning. Raul had been unable to identify the guy back in Matamoros and was stunned by my unexpected encounter back home. I told him I was certain it was the same guy. But without a photo of the man, neither of us was sure what to do next. Raul promised to keep investigating him.

After breakfast with my girls, I went to meet with Craig Kinney, Joe's financial adviser at Austin Wealth Capital. As the executor of Joe's estate, I needed to get the rundown on my father-in-law's financial situation and begin to sort out what he wanted to do with his money in the event of his death. And how to best take care of my mother-in-law moving forward. This was not a surprise to Carol. She had agreed that I'd handle things when Joe had set this in place several years ago. Of course, none of us believed it would be necessary for many decades.

Austin Wealth Capital had expansive offices on the fourteenth floor of the Frost Bank Tower in the heart of downtown. I rode up in a crowded elevator and noticed that one of the guys in the carriage with me had a small tattoo of crossed cannons on his left wrist. I knew the tattoo was popular in the navy. My father, who had also served on the seas in his youth, had something similar inked on his right bicep. Thinking about my dad and then about Joe hit me hard. I'd now lost the two most important men in my life.

I got out on the fourteenth floor. Craig was a balding, sixtysomething man with glasses, a beard, and a black suit. He looked like someone you could trust with your money. I'd never met the man but knew that Joe had been with him for a long time. We sat down in his spacious corner office. After offering my family and me his deepest condolences, he took a file from his desktop and handed it to me.

"I pulled everything together first thing this morning after getting your call."

For the next fifteen minutes, Craig gave me a full summary of all Joe's financial investments and accounts. As expected, my father-in-law had done quite well as an attorney over the years. Carol should be set for the rest of her life. But I was surprised, considering how much money he'd invested into our startup business, that his overall net worth was not much higher than what it currently showed on his financial portfolio. Something was clearly missing. And it was an important something.

"Craig, where's a listing for the money that Joe invested in my company three years ago? I don't see it anywhere in here."

The bald man pitched his head. "What money?"

I looked up at him. "The five million dollars."

Craig's eyebrows bunched. "Five million?"

"Why do you seem surprised?"

"Because this is the first I've heard of it, Alex. I wasn't aware Joe had invested in your company. He never told me anything."

"What? Are you serious?"

"I am. Where did he get the money?"

"Joe said it was settlement money or something from a client from years ago that he'd set aside somewhere."

"Five million?" Craig repeated, the pitch of his voice elevated.

"Yes," I confirmed. "Probably more. Joe mentioned he could go back to it if my company ever needed it. How could you not know about it?"

Craig eased back in his office chair, elbows on his armrests, his fingers laced together under his chin. "I don't know what to say. I'm baffled. Joe's been my client for nearly ten years. This is the first time I've heard about money of that kind of magnitude being set aside somewhere. It doesn't make a lot of sense to me. Are you sure he said it was settlement money from an old case?"

It was my turn to sit back and think. Was I sure? I rewound a scene from three years ago in my mind and tried hard to remember exactly what Joe had said the night that had changed damn near everything for Taylor and me.

By the time I'd finally walked through the garage door inside our three-bedroom South Austin home, I'd been completely exhausted. I'd been traveling all week, working my way up the East Coast through places like Philadelphia, New York, and Boston. I'd put in long hours, giving the same presentation over and over again, living off fast food, and sleeping every night in uncomfortable hotel beds. This had been my life for the past couple of years. And I was so tired of it. Olivia was already four, Nicole was two, and I was missing pretty much everything while they grew up way too fast. Something had to change. We had talked about my starting something of my own, either as a consultant or maybe even a new company, but the potential for sudden dramatic loss of income felt way too risky.

I set my luggage down in the back hallway and could hear my family around the corner in the kitchen. Olivia was laughing hard about something. This instantly brought a smile to my face. I couldn't wait to scoop her and Nicole into my arms. I also knew that my in-laws were here because Joe's Mercedes was parked out front. Taylor's parents spent a lot of time at our house when I was traveling. We really appreciated the extra help. Although I'm not sure helping to manage my household was what Joe had in mind when he retired from his law practice a couple of years ago.

Stepping into the kitchen, I was greeted with squeals of "Daddy! Daddy!" when both of my girls placed eyes on me. They raced around the kitchen island and jumped into my arms with total confidence that I would catch them both. I did and squeezed them tightly.

"Hi, girls." I sat them down, kissed both of them repeatedly on the foreheads. "So good to see you."

Olivia and Nicole immediately started talking on top of each other, wanting to tell me every story they could possibly remember over the past few days. They were already in their pajamas. It was nearing their bedtime. I did my best to listen, but my eyes were already on Taylor, who leaned against the counter, gave me a tired grin, and waited her turn. When the girls took their first breaths, I walked over to my wife and gave her a quick kiss. She put her arms around my neck.

"How was your flight?" she asked me.

"Same as all the others."

"Well, I'm glad you're home. I have some leftovers in the fridge, if you're hungry. My dad grilled cheeseburgers for us."

"Okay, thanks. I'm starving."

Carol welcomed me back, and Joe offered to pour me a glass of bourbon, like he was drinking. I gladly accepted.

I turned back to Taylor. "Why does it feel so warm in here?"

She frowned. "AC is acting up again."

"Are you serious?"

We'd just dropped a grand we didn't have to get it fixed two weeks ago.

"Been going off and on all day today," Taylor explained.

I felt a surge of anger. "I'm going to rip that AC guy a new one."

"Settle down. You just got home. Besides, maybe there's a bright side."

I tilted my head at her. "What's that?"

She leaned into my ear, whispered, "We may have to sleep naked tonight."

We shared a quick hidden smile.

"Silver linings," I whispered back. "Maybe we should leave it broken for a while."

She laughed, kissed me again.

The girls were back inside our circle, showing me drawings, paintings, crafts—basically, everything they'd created over the past five days. I did my best to try to pay attention to the story behind each one, but my mind was still on Taylor. While I hated being away from the girls so much, I definitely missed my wife.

Joe returned with my glass of bourbon. "Can I talk to you for a moment, Alex?"

"Of course."

I followed him out the back sliding door to our small patio. We didn't have much of a backyard, but there was enough for a playscape. Taylor and I had hoped to buy a bigger house by now with a more spacious yard for the girls, but the promotions I'd been promised had still not come through for me. Taylor had even mentioned trying to go back to work somehow to afford a bigger mortgage, but we weren't sure how she could possibly pull that off with me out on the road so much. We were both frustrated.

I shut the sliding door behind me and sat in a lawn chair opposite Joe. I could hear a neighbor's kid playing his music too loud next door. I took a swig of the bourbon, tried to allow the alcohol to drown out my annoyance.

"Long trip?" Joe asked me.

"They're all long right now, Joe."

"I can tell it's wearing on you."

"Taylor, too. She has it much harder than me."

"Tough stage of life with little ones at home. Maybe I can help."

"You already watch the girls several days a week."

"I'm talking about financially."

I looked over at him. "What do you mean?"

"Well, Taylor mentioned you guys had been talking about starting a company of your own. She said you had even discussed numbers to show investors, but you were uneasy about the risk. I'd like to take away that uneasiness."

"That was just fantasy talk, Joe. I can't take your money."

"Why not? I've had something set aside from an old client case from way back. We could treat it like an investment."

"That's really nice of you, but we're not talking about a couple hundred thousand dollars. It would take something much more serious to really get this kind of company off the ground in the right way."

"Millions?"

"Probably," I said, laughing it off, finishing my bourbon.

"Then count me in."

My head whipped back around to him. I fully expected to see a joking smile on my father-in-law's face. But he was looking at me deadpan.

"Joe?"

"Like I said, I've had something set aside for a long time. Looking at you and Taylor, the girls, I think it's time for me to put that money to good use."

"I'm certain," I told Craig. "Joe said it was from a client case. Could he have possibly been working with another financial planner?"

"Doubtful. The whole point of wealth management is to create a *complete* road map for an individual or a family to reach their goals. Leaving millions of dollars out of the picture would be an odd and, forgive for me saying, stupid thing to do. And Joe Dobson was not stupid."

Craig was right. Joe was incredibly smart. So why was his own financial adviser unaware of the money? I again thought about the encounter last night with the intruder from Mexico. He hadn't stolen anything. But he was clearly there searching for something. Could it have somehow been connected to the money?

ELEVEN

I left the Frost Bank Tower feeling more uneasy than when I'd entered and walked two blocks north up Congress Avenue to the Littlefield Building, where my software company, Illuminate, occupied the entire fifth floor. At Illuminate, we specialized in online presentation tools for companies that needed creative videos and PowerPoints but didn't want to start from scratch or hire staff. Upon arriving, I said a quick hello to the receptionist and some of the staff. We currently had a team of forty that included software engineers, designers, sales and marketing teams, and a couple of other support staff. We were in the process of trying to hire a dozen more team members to keep up with the rapid growth. I followed a hallway to the corner, where my glass office sat right next to the office of Mark Groutas, our chief financial officer. Mark and I had gone to college together at UT, where he was on the swim team. Tall and lean, Mark was a brilliant CPA and had masterfully used our initial investment money to grow us quickly.

As usual, his face was buried in his laptop. But he looked up when I entered. "Hey, what're you doing here? I thought you were going to take the rest of the week off."

"I am. Just stopped in for a second."

"Well, it's good to see you, bud. How's Taylor doing?"

"Up and down. But you know Taylor. She can always put on a strong face."

"Yeah. And what about you? You and Joe were super tight."

"I'm not going to lie, man, I'm feeling crushed. He meant so much to me."

"To all of us, obviously. Take as much time off as you need. I've got things covered around here. We're all grieving along with you."

"I appreciate it. Speaking of Joe, can you look up from where he wired us the startup money three years ago?"

"Of course. What's going on?"

"I'm just trying to sort out some of his financials."

Mark began typing on his keyboard and squinted at his laptop screen. "The money came in from Pioneer Bank."

"The entire sum?"

He nodded. "Yes. One large transaction. Don't you remember? We barely had, like, a thousand bucks in the account, and then it all changed overnight."

"Yeah, that was quite the day."

I opened the financial folder that Craig Kinney had given me on my father-in-law and scanned through the paperwork. Joe's main bank was Wells Fargo. There was no mention of Pioneer Bank anywhere in the folder. Why had Joe used a different bank?

I left the office and drove straight to a Pioneer Bank branch near my neighborhood. A thirtysomething brunette banker named Missy warmly greeted me and invited me back to her desk cubicle just off the main lobby.

"How can I help you?" she offered.

"My father-in-law has an account here. He passed away a few days ago. As the executor of his estate, I'm trying to sort out his financial situation and hoped to get some information from you."

"Certainly. I'm so sorry for your loss."

"Thank you."

"Do you have an official letter of testamentary?"

"Not yet. Working on it. But I have a copy of his Last Will and Testament. I'm not looking to do anything with his money today. I just need information."

I showed her the paperwork I'd carried with me, along with my driver's license. She began to type on her computer.

"It actually doesn't look like Mr. Dobson still has an account with us. He closed it three years ago."

"For how long was his account here open?"

She again examined her computer monitor. "Only for a week. He opened it with a transfer, wired the money back out, and then he proceeded to close his account. All in the same week."

"One transfer?" I asked her.

She nodded. "Yes. One in, one out."

"Five million dollars?"

She looked over at me. "Correct."

That was odd. Joe had opened the account here only to wire the initial investment money in and out to us. Why? "Can you tell me from where the money originated?"

More typing from Missy. "An investment bank called Wallow House."

"Wallow House? Where is that?"

She squinted at her screen. "Cayman Islands."

I pitched my head. Why would Joe have kept money in the Caymans?

"Are there any other names attached to the transfer?"

"Just one," she replied. "Ethan Tucker."

I recognized the name. Joe had just mentioned Ethan the night before our trip to Mexico. It was the first time I'd heard my father-in-law say anything about him.

All our luggage pieces had been opened on the bed. Taylor was busy folding clothes—for her and both of the girls—and placing them inside the luggage, while I did my usual last-minute scramble to gather whatever I felt like I needed. I drove her crazy with my frenzied approach to trips. I could hear Olivia and Nicole in the living room, singing as loud as they could while they put on a song-and-dance performance for Joe and Carol. Based off their costumes, tonight's show was all about Frozen II. Olivia was dressed as Anna, and Nicole was Elsa. I could hear my youngest belting out "Into the Unknown." I was afraid she might burst a vocal cord.

I could feel a headache coming on quickly. My in-laws had come over a few minutes ago to help watch the girls while we tried to finish packing. It was nearly impossible to pack with them jumping all over the bed and pulling stuff in and out of their little pink suitcases. Like trying to brush your teeth while eating Oreo cookies. We were grateful for the extra help.

"It's going to be hard to put them down tonight," Taylor said. "They've been bouncing off the walls about the trip all day."

"I'm glad they're excited."

"You might not feel that way when they're still up at midnight."

I laughed. "Maybe we should send them home with your parents tonight."

She shook her head. "I don't think we should do that to my parents."

"Why not? Isn't that what grandparents are for? Dumping kids?" I sidled up next to her, placed a pair of my old running shoes inside my suitcase. Then I moved in behind her, wrapped my arms around her waist, kissed her on the neck. "Besides, we could use a night alone. We're about to have two restless kids in our bed for the next week."

She smiled. "That's true."

I kissed her again, went back into our bathroom.

"You packed our passports, right?" Taylor called after me.

"Of course," I replied. Then I doubted myself. "I'd better double-check," I said, crossing through the bedroom again.

She rolled her eyes at me. "Yeah, you'd better. I'd hate to make you drive all the way back here tomorrow by yourself."

Walking through the living room, I smiled at my girls, who were dancing in front of our big fireplace while Joe and Carol sat on the sofa and watched. Olivia and Nicole begged me to also stop and watch, but I told them I had to keep getting things together for our big day tomorrow. I was also excited about bringing them down to the orphanage. We had done several family trips together the past couple of years—Disney World, skiing in Colorado, the Bahamas—but this was something entirely different. I had high hopes that being with less-fortunate kids their age might help my girls realize how blessed we were as a family. Life had been so good to us the past couple of years. We needed to share that goodness with others. I was also glad that Joe and Carol had wanted to come with us. Joe had a big heart for those in need. I had a good feeling about this trip.

Stepping into my home office, I walked around my desk and pulled open the middle drawer. Sure enough, I'd forgotten to pack our passports. They were sitting in the drawer wrapped up in a rubber band. I shook my head, rolled my eyes at myself. Saved again by my wife—story of my life. I pulled them out, checked to make sure I also had the girls covered, and then closed the drawer.

Joe stepped inside my office with me. "Wow, the girls are really wired tonight."

I laughed. "You think?"

"You want them to stay with us? Carol has a way of getting them down more easily."

"You mean bribing them with sweets?"

Joe smiled, shrugged. "Whatever it takes, right?"

"You read my mind. I just mentioned that possibility to Taylor."

"Great. I'll start rounding them up and get them out of your hair."

I began to move past him into the hallway, but Joe stopped me with a hand on my shoulder. "Hey, are you sure about this trip? I'm second-guessing it."

I pitched my head. "Why?"

"Maybe Taylor is right. It can be dangerous across the border. Maybe we should reconsider. Plus, I've got a case I really need to work on here this next week."

"Come on, Joe, I think we'll be fine. But if you need to stay back to work, it's no problem. I can take care of everything myself."

"Are you sure?"

"Of course. But you're going to have to tell the girls yourself. They're going to be crushed that you're not coming with us. They've been looking forward to it for weeks."

Joe sighed, rubbed the back of his neck for a moment. "Who am I kidding? I can't be away from the girls for an entire week."

I smiled. "I'm glad to hear you say that. We're going to have fun."

"It was dumb of me to even think about it." His forehead wrinkled a touch. "But just as a precaution, I've shown you where I keep all of my personal financial info at the house, right?"

"Yeah. Top drawer of your file cabinet."

He nodded. "Right. And you know to go see Craig Kinney if anything was ever to, you know, happen?"

"Yes."

"Good. One more thing. Have I ever mentioned my, uh, old friend Ethan to you?"

"I don't think so." My eyes narrowed. "Joe, what's up? Aren't you being a little paranoid? We're not traveling to a war zone. We're going to be fine."

But my father-in-law didn't get the opportunity to expound because Olivia and Nicole had tracked him down. The girls grabbed him on both arms, trying to drag him back to the living room to keep watching their performance. My girls were a force to reckon with when they wanted something.

Joe looked at me, forced a smile. "It's nothing, really. It can wait."

That entire brief exchange with Joe felt eerie now in light of everything that had unfolded afterward.

"Is there any contact info for Ethan Tucker?" I asked Missy.

"There's a phone number listed on the transaction. Do you want it?"

"Yes, I do, thanks."

Missy wrote it down on a sticky note for me. After walking out of the bank, I sat in my Tahoe in the parking lot and stared at the phone number. A 214 area code—Dallas. I pulled out my cell phone and quickly called the number. Disconnected. Sighing, I sat back in my car seat. Five million from an offshore account in the Cayman Islands? Did Joe have more money there? If so, how much? I again thought about what Joe had said the other night before our trip. He almost pulled out of the trip at the last minute, which was so unlike him. He then wanted to make sure I knew what to do in the event of his death. Did he know he was in some kind of danger? Is that why he didn't look shocked when those men grabbed him? Was his abduction not random?

I needed to track down Ethan Tucker ASAP.

TWELVE

When I got home, Olivia and Nicole were outside in the pool, splashing around on an oversize mermaid float. It was good to see them laughing today. There had been a lot of tears last night while tucking them into bed. If possible, I wanted them to somehow enjoy their last few weeks of summer before school started. Carol was sitting in the shade on the back patio, watching the girls with Lizzie in her lap. Taylor was in the kitchen, making peanut butter-and-jelly sandwiches and cutting up strawberries and bananas. I felt unsure what to share with her about what I'd discovered this morning. It was still a lot of speculation. I didn't want to unnecessarily freak her out when she was already emotionally taxed. At least not until I'd had a chance to chase down Ethan Tucker and see if I could figure this thing out first. Still, I didn't like withholding information from her. She could usually tell.

I walked over and kissed her on the cheek.

"Hey," she said. "How'd it go with Craig Kinney?"

"Uh, good. As expected, your mom is completely set. She'll never have to worry about money. Your dad made sure of that."

"So you think she'll be able to stay in their house?"

"Yes, I do. If that's what she wants."

"That's a relief. Although I'll probably have to teach her how to pay her mortgage now that . . ."

Taylor's words trailed off. I remembered that feeling well. Of not wanting to acknowledge reality in the immediate aftermath of my own father's death. It felt too damn hard to say out loud that he was gone. Taylor paused for only a moment, took a breath, and continued to slice strawberries.

"How's your mom doing today?" I asked.

"Okay, I guess. She's still not talking much about it. She actually snapped at me earlier when I mentioned something about Dad to the girls."

"Give her time. She'll come around."

"I hope so. Thanks again for getting Lizzie. I did see a brief smile on my mom's face this morning when she came out of her bedroom and Lizzie raced over to her. And, of course, the girls were overjoyed."

"Maybe we should consider getting them a dog now," I suggested. *Now*, of course, meaning to fill the sudden void in our lives. Taylor had resisted getting a dog because she knew she would have to do most of the work of dealing with a pet at home on top of everything else on her plate. So I hadn't pushed.

"Maybe," she replied but didn't take it any further. "My mom wants to have Dad's service as soon as possible. I called over to the church. We can do it this Saturday afternoon. Pastor Larsen is available. He sends his regards."

"Saturday is quick."

"My mom thinks it's better for everyone, so the healing can begin. Anyway, Joslin at the church said they'd handle everything and get the word out. She asked me if we wanted to put together some kind of video presentation with pictures of my dad, but I'm not sure I have it in me right now to go through all of our family photos."

"I'll do it," I offered.

"Thank you." She walked to the fridge and pulled it open. "Can you please tell the girls to get dried off for lunch?"

"Sure."

I walked out onto the patio and called for the girls to get out of the pool. They ignored me and kept on playing. It always took me four or five tries before they'd finally listen. So I sat in a patio chair next to my mother-in-law.

"Lizzie seems happy," I said.

I smiled at the dog. I had stopped by the neighbor's house earlier this morning to pay the teenage dog sitter and ask her about the house alarm. She said she'd made sure to set it every night when she left. If that was true—and who knows for sure with teenagers—that meant the intruder from last night had somehow disarmed it. And disarming complex alarm systems was not the mark of a common criminal.

"Thank you for bringing her over, Alex. I hope it's not too much trouble having Lizzie around here."

"No trouble at all. We love her. Did you get any rest last night?"

"Some."

"Good. Carol, can I ask you a question about your financials?"

"Of course."

"I went to see Craig Kinney this morning."

"Craig is a sweet man. So is his wife, Marcy."

"He sends his condolences. We went over your finances. I just wanted to get a jump start to make sure you're in good shape. Everything looks very solid, by the way. You should have no concerns. But Craig didn't seem to know where Joe got the money that he invested in my company. It wasn't part of your financial portfolio. Do you have any idea why Joe would've kept that money separate from his other finances?"

"No, but I'm sure Joe had a good reason. He was always very particular when it came to our money."

"Did Joe ever mention anything about an account in the Cayman Islands?"

Carol shook her head. "Joe never wanted me to be too involved or concerned with our money. He always said it was his role to carry that burden. So I let him all these years. I'm sorry that's not much help to you now."

"It's okay. What about the name Ethan Tucker?"

"Doesn't sound familiar."

"Do you remember anything about the lawsuit settlement where Joe got the money he put into my company?"

"What lawsuit settlement?"

"Joe told me he got the money from a client case a long time ago."

"Oh, I didn't know that. But if you want to know about a particular case, you should probably talk to Steve Edmonds."

Steve Edmonds had been Joe's law partner for nearly twenty years before they shut down their firm a few years ago when Joe wanted to retire.

"Where is Steve these days?"

"He joined one of those big firms. I can't remember the name of it. Joe called it a meat market. Do you want me to call his wife, Cindy, and find out?"

"No, that's okay. I'll find him."

After rallying the girls inside for lunch, I shut the pocket doors to my home office, circled my desk, and sat in the high-dollar executive chair my in-laws had purchased for me as a gift this past Christmas. It was one of those fancy ergonomic numbers that perfectly supported all areas of my back. Joe had bought one for himself. After commenting how much I liked it, I found one waiting for me by the Christmas tree with a big red bow on it. That's just how my father-in-law always worked. He'd pull his shirt right off the moment I needed it. He'd drop everything to come help me fix a water leak. He'd spend his whole weekend assisting me with installing new landscape lighting. I could always count on Joe.

Sliding open the middle drawer of my desk, I found where I'd stored Joe's cell phone. After powering it up, I began scrolling through his contacts for the name Ethan Tucker. Joe had called him an *old friend*. So I was surprised when I came up empty-handed. Joe did not have the name in his phone.

Opening my laptop on my desk, I did a quick search grouping Joe Dobson with Ethan Tucker. But nothing appeared with that direct connection. I hopped onto LinkedIn and searched for Ethan Tucker in Dallas. Several matches popped up, including candidates like a lawyer, an accountant, a banker, and a financial adviser. I started with the lawyer, searched online for the law firm where he worked, found the main phone number listed on their website, and made my first cold call. A friendly woman answered.

"Clareview and Marshall, how can I help you?"

"Hi, I need to speak with Ethan Tucker, please."

"May I ask who's calling?"

I thought about that for a moment, then said, "Joe Dobson."

I figured if this was the same Ethan Tucker who'd wired the money, giving my father-in-law's name might actually get me on the phone with him. Otherwise, I could easily get brushed off. I didn't want that to happen.

"One moment," she replied.

I stared at the lawyer's profile page on the firm's website. He was probably in his midforties. Curly hair and kind of pudgy. Undergrad at Virginia Tech. Law school at Georgetown. Specialized in corporate securities.

A few seconds later, the guy was on the phone. "This is Ethan."

His subdued greeting led me to believe he didn't know my father-in-law. There was not a hint of recognition. Still, I pressed forward.

"Ethan, this is Joe Dobson. How are you?"

"I'm fine. Do I, uh, know you, Joe?"

"Well, you should. You wired me five million dollars three years ago."

I said it with a casual chuckle, trying to be disarming. But he didn't bite.

"Uh, I'm sorry, but I think you've got the wrong guy here."

"Wallow House. The Caymans. Does that ring a bell?"

"No, it doesn't."

I believed him. I quickly apologized and hung up. I moved on to candidate number two and did the same thing with an accountant named Ethan Tucker who worked at a big firm. I called the main line and got put through to him. But the results were about the same. This guy clearly didn't know anything about my father-in-law. I moved on to the banker but only got a voice mail. I would try again later. I finally hit up Ethan Tucker the financial adviser, who was a partner at Lone Star Financial. The firm's website showed a gray-haired man who was probably around the same age as my father-in-law. He'd earned a finance degree from Southern Methodist University and then a master's degree from Wharton. I again ran through my spiel with the receptionist and claimed to be Joe Dobson.

I knew I had something the moment he got on the phone with me. The man spoke with a hushed urgency. "Damn, Joe. It's been over a week already. And why the hell are you calling my work phone and not my cell phone?"

"Ethan, this is not Joe. My name is Alex Mahan."

"What . . . Who?"

"I'm Joe's son-in-law."

He paused, then: "What is this about?"

"I had some questions I was hoping you could answer for me."

"What kind of questions?"

"Well, three years ago, you wired my father-in-law five million dollars from an offshore account in the Caymans—"

"Who told you that?" he abruptly interrupted.

"The bank did. I just wanted to know—"

He interrupted me again, clearly agitated. "Why're you calling me?"

"Like I said, I have questions about this money because my father-in-law invested it in my company. I'm looking for the rest of it."

"Then ask your father-in-law."

"Joe died a couple of days ago."

Another pause. "How?"

"He was abducted and killed while we were on a trip to Mexico."

Ethan cursed. I found it unusual that Ethan had waited to express himself this way until *after* hearing how Joe had died. Was I reading too much into that?

"How did you know Joe?" I asked him.

The tone of his voice softened. "I can't talk about this with you, Alex. This is . . . dangerous."

"What? Why?"

"Look, I'm truly sorry for your loss. I am. Joe was, uh . . . I, uh, I gotta go."

"Wait? I need to know more about that money."

The phone line went dead. I couldn't believe it. He'd hung up on me. Why? It was the second time in the past twelve hours someone had hung up on me in the middle of a conversation about Joe's death. Irritated, I again called Ethan's financial firm, pretended to be someone else with the receptionist, just to see if I could somehow get the man back on the phone. I thought about how Ethan had answered my first call: *Damn, Joe. It's been more than a week already.* He had clearly spoken with my father-in-law recently. About what? Was it related to the money? After placing me on hold, the receptionist came back on the phone and told me that Ethan would unfortunately be out of the office the rest of the afternoon. I hung up in frustration.

Why had the man said talking to me was dangerous?

What the hell was going on?

THIRTEEN

On my way to meet with Steve Edmonds, I made a quick stop at my in-laws' house to see if I could find anything in Joe's home files related to Ethan Tucker or the mystery account in the Cayman Islands. Entering through the garage, I paused in the back hallway and listened for any noise inside the house. I was still very much on edge after last night's altercation. Thankfully, all seemed quiet.

Walking the length of the house, I stepped up to Joe's home office. I stopped for a brief moment in the entryway, feeling a sudden rush of emotions. I was so used to seeing Joe sitting in his office chair behind his desk, reading glasses on, paperwork in his hands. It was hard to believe I never would again. Standing there, I could actually smell my father-in-law's fragrance in the room. Like a mix of Old Spice, bourbon, and cigars. I always loved that smell. To me, Joe always smelled like success.

I moved to the three drawers of files that were built into the wall of wood shelves behind Joe's desk. Pulling out each file, I began searching. Most were files for my in-laws' personal matters. Mortgage information. Tax records. Utilities. Bills and so forth. There were a few client files for cases Joe must've been currently handling. But in all my searching, I could find nothing about Ethan Tucker or the Cayman Islands.

Maybe his former law partner could help me out.

Steve Edmonds was a senior partner at Tolstoy & Myers, a big corporate law firm that occupied two floors near the top of the thirty-story One Eleven Congress building. I knew him pretty well because he and Joe had been partners for nearly twenty years. Steve and his wife were around for a lot of family functions and parties. But I hadn't seen or spoken with him since they'd broken up their little firm five years ago. From what I knew, it was not a bad breakup. Joe just told me the two men wanted to go in different directions. Steve was ten years younger and still full of healthy ambition. Joe wanted to start taking some steps back and make more time for his grandkids. So they dissolved their law firm of two partners, two associates, and a couple of support staff, then went their own ways.

Steve met me in the firm's lobby. Short and overweight, he had black hair that was graying on the sides and wore khaki pants and a long-sleeve white dress shirt. We shared a handshake and then a quick hug.

Steve's face sagged. "I can't believe this, Alex. This is the worst news ever. I can't even focus today; I'm so shook up by it. Joe meant the world to me."

"We're all shook up by it. It's been a really tough couple of days."

"I can't even imagine. Carol must be distraught."

"She's hanging in there."

"When is the service?"

"Saturday. I'll get you the details."

"You know I'll be there in the front row. Joe was my mentor. I pretty much owe everything I am as a lawyer to him. Hell, as a man."

"I feel the same way."

"Let's go back to my office to talk. Can I get you anything? Coffee? Soda? Maybe something stronger? I know I'll need it to handle this news today."

"I'm fine, thanks."

I followed Steve down a busy hallway lined with lawyers, paralegals, and assistants and into a spacious partner's office that had a desk on one side and a small sitting area with a leather sofa and two chairs on the other side. Steve invited me to sit on the sofa while he squeezed himself into one of the chairs next to me.

"You said on the phone you had some questions about Joe's old cases?" Steve said.

"I do. I've started sorting out Joe's financials, and I'm having a difficult time piecing a couple of things together. Three years ago, Joe invested a lot of money to help me start my company, Illuminate."

"I heard about that. I spoke briefly with Joe a few months ago. He mentioned how well your company was doing and seemed very proud of you and Taylor. Congratulations."

"Thanks. At the time of the investment, Joe told me the money he was putting into the company came from a big client case he'd set aside years ago. I was curious if you knew anything about that."

"How much money? If you don't mind my asking."

"Five million dollars."

Steve's square head jerked back a bit. "What? Five million?"

"You're surprised?"

"I am. I think the biggest settlement Joe and I ever won was for around seven hundred thousand dollars—which, of course, we split with our client. Are you sure he said it came from one of his old cases?"

"Positive. And he said there was more available should my company need it to continue to grow."

Steve's chubby forehead bunched up. "Damn. That's *a lot* of money. Well, it definitely didn't come from any case while we worked together. Plus, that kind of case doesn't even sound like the Joe I knew."

"What do you mean?"

"Joe stayed away from the big-money, high-profile cases. I always wanted to go after them, to make a bigger name for ourselves, to reel in even bigger fish, but Joe always wanted us to turn them down. He said he didn't want the headaches and the stress."

"Joe was a wise man."

"Yes, he was. I wish I had one more chance to tell him that."

I thought about what Steve had just said. "So do you think this big case could've happened before you guys were together?"

Steve leaned back in his chair, rested his hands on his belly. "I suppose. But why would Joe never mention it to me? I mean, we were together for almost twenty years. You swap a hell of a lot of stories when you are in a small office together for that long. In many ways, I felt like I knew him even better than I knew Cindy. But Joe never said a single word about a settlement like that."

"Yeah, it doesn't make sense. Do you know someone named Ethan Tucker?"

He shook his head. "Who is he?"

"He wired the money that Joe invested in my company."

"You know, I still share a storage unit with Joe where we kept all of our old boxes of case files. Joe had plenty of boxes in there from before we ever formed our firm together. If there's something to this case settlement, I bet it would be in there somewhere. If you want, I can give you the security codes. You're welcome to go check it out for yourself."

"Thanks. I will."

I left Steve's office more troubled than when I'd entered. Why wouldn't Joe have mentioned a settlement that substantial to his law partner of twenty years? Lawyers were known for bragging about their big wins. Although Joe was humbler than most, it still seemed like something that would come up at some point. And why was Carol completely oblivious to the whole thing? If Joe had won a case that big early in his career—one that resulted in him pocketing a whopping $5 million or more—wouldn't he have celebrated the win with his wife? I wondered if that meant the case predated their marriage. Even so, wouldn't Joe have said something to Carol if he'd won a case that put millions in the bank before they were married? But he didn't.

I could feel my anxiety steadily growing.

Maybe I'd find something in the storage unit.

Headed down the elevator with a small crowd of others, I began searching Google on my phone to see if anything might pop up online in relation to Joe Dobson and a big case settlement. It was a shot in the dark if the case was from before he had his firm with Steve. There were little news snippets here and there about cases involving Joe, but most of them were much more recent and on a small scale. Nothing at all jumped out about a multimillion-dollar settlement.

When the elevator doors opened in the lobby, I mindlessly walked out with the others, my face still planted in my phone. As I turned a corner, I bumped into someone coming from the opposite direction. It wasn't a hard bump but enough to make me look up and immediately begin to apologize. The other party did the same. A brief "Sorry, sorry" exchange. But then I did a double take as the man moved past me. He was probably in his midfifties, bald with a brown mustache, wearing a tan, short-sleeve button-down shirt and jeans. He was the same guy with the navy tattoo on his wrist who had been inside the elevator with me this morning when I was going to see Craig Kinney. I watched him as he entered an elevator with a group of others. When he turned around, his eyes were directly on me. And they remained locked on me until the elevator doors completely shut.

Something told me it wasn't a coincidence.

FOURTEEN

The storage unit was on the second floor of a nice facility just a few miles outside of downtown. I punched in the security codes Steve had given me to access the property gate and the building, then found a red metal garage-style door marked *213* halfway down a long hallway. After plugging in the numbers on the lock, I pulled the garage door all the way up and peered inside. The unit was probably ten feet by fifteen feet. As Steve had said, it was filled with stacks of old legal boxes. There were probably more than a hundred. I shook my head. Lawyers could create a lot of paperwork.

Thankfully, they'd left a walkway in the middle of the unit to access whichever box they needed. Those stacked in the very front were a crisper white and clearly from their most recent cases. All of them had black marker written on the outside identifying them by case name and date, and tagging them with either Steve's or Joe's name. Based on my conversation with Steve, I figured there was no real reason to search any of the boxes dated from their time working together. So I moved all the way to the back of the unit, where I found the oldest boxes. About twenty of them were stacked up against the back wall. They were well worn, some smashed in slightly on one corner or another, and a few were stained from either coffee or other unidentified liquids. Most of these boxes were also marked on the outside with case information.

I pulled a box from the top, set it on the floor, and lifted off the lid. It was stuffed with manila folders. I yanked one out and opened it. Joe's name was on all the paperwork. I knew he had worked on his own for a while before forming his firm with Steve. The dates showed that the case was from more than thirty years ago. Was it necessary to keep legal paperwork forever? I skimmed that particular file and then pulled out another one. I wasn't exactly sure what I was looking for—I wasn't a lawyer, after all—but I figured something might stand out to me if Joe had landed a case with a huge potential settlement.

I closed the first box without success and moved on to the next, where I found basically a match of the other with dozens of manila folders. I took a deep breath and let it out slowly. This could take a while. For the next hour or so, I quickly rummaged through so much legal paperwork that my eyes began to blur. I had no idea how attorneys did this every day. I'd go stir-crazy. Twenty boxes into my search, I still had not found *anything* that indicated Joe had at some point won a big case worth millions of dollars.

Tiring, I grabbed one of the boxes near the bottom of the stack and yanked off the lid. It was pretty much the same as with all the others. Manila folders with mind-numbing legal paperwork. But there were different attorney names listed: Bruce Gibson and Daniel Gibson, Attorneys-at-Law. I started pulling files out and quickly skimmed them. Joe's name was not mentioned anywhere. I wondered why Joe had a box with someone else's files. I pulled out another box and found that it also belonged to the same attorneys. Inside one folder, I didn't find any legal paperwork; instead, I found a standard white mailing envelope with Joe's name and an address in Vancouver handwritten on the outside. I knew Vancouver was where Joe and Carol had met and gotten married before they'd decided to move to Texas when my mother-in-law was pregnant with Taylor. There was no return address written on the envelope.

Opening it, I discovered a letter inside along with a small color photograph of a very attractive young blonde woman wearing a red dress and sitting on a park bench with what looked like the Washington Monument behind her. I flipped the photograph over. Nothing was written on the back. I unfolded the letter. A date scribbled at the top indicated it was written nearly thirty-four years ago. However, even though the envelope had Joe's name on it, the letter was actually addressed to Daniel. I presumed it was the same Daniel from Bruce Gibson and Daniel Gibson, Attorneys-at-Law.

> *Daniel,*
> *These past few weeks have been the hardest of my life. I miss you like crazy. I can't believe this is the path we've been forced to take. But like we've always said, c'est la vie. Life really isn't fair sometimes. I know we are supposed to cut things completely off between us, but everything felt so rushed there at the end. Please know you'll forever have a special place in my heart. I will always consider you my husband. I can only pray that life will show us mercy and one day allow us to be together again.*
> *Love, Greta*

I stared at the name at the bottom. Greta? I immediately thought about the strange text messages that had arrived on Joe's phone the past couple of days. Could this be the same person? It seemed likely. Greta was not a common name. The photograph showed her to be in DC, which was the location where the other Greta had texted my father-in-law. I again wondered about Joe's recent trip to attend the DC legal conference. What was the name of the conference again? I remembered my father-in-law saying something to Carol while we were all out to dinner together. The conference had to do with nonprofit organizations. Joe did a lot of pro bono work for local nonprofits.

On my phone, I began to search for DC legal conferences involving nonprofits. I scanned the search results until I found the exact name he'd mentioned at dinner the other night: Washington Nonprofit Legal & Tax Conference. I clicked on the link, brought up the conference's home page, and then cursed out loud. The conference wasn't scheduled until this coming October—three months from now. Joe had lied about it.

I looked at the photograph of the attractive young woman again.

So why had he really gone to DC ten days ago?

FIFTEEN

I drove home feeling completely stressed. Where the hell had Joe gotten the money he'd invested in my company? Was it connected to his death? Were the two strange men I'd run into over the past few days also looking for it? My chest started tightening at the thought of how everything Taylor and I had built together these past three years—the new house, the pool, the nice cars, the private schools, the trips, our entire future—might somehow be connected to something dangerous.

When I got home, the girls were in the backyard on the swing set. Carol was taking turns pushing both of them. Nicole was my little daredevil. She kept yelling for Nanny to push her higher and higher. Her older sister was much more reserved. I could see that Olivia had her fingers fiercely gripped on the chains with a concerned look on her face. But she would never admit to being scared. I noticed a slight smile on my mother-in-law's face as my girls squealed with glee. Then I thought about what I'd discovered about Joe's trip to DC and felt knots in my stomach. Did my mother-in-law suspect anything? I also pondered why Carol had been kept so out of the loop when it came to their financial situation. Could Joe have intentionally kept his wife at a distance with their money because there was something more to it?

Taylor and I had never operated that way. Every part of our home and work lives were wrapped up together. Taylor paid most of our personal bills and knew every dollar in each of our bank accounts. There was nothing hidden between us when it came to our money. It was only after we'd had kids that my income became our sole income. She'd had a rock-star marketing career going when she became pregnant with Olivia. The initial plan had been for her to take a brief work break when Olivia was young and then get back out there. She enjoyed what she did. But then she got pregnant right away with Nicole. The brief break turned into something much more extended. With both girls now in school full-time, we had been talking about her doing some consultant work. We didn't need the money—far from it. But Taylor mentioned she wanted to put some of her energy into more than just our home and the girls.

I found Taylor folding clothes in the laundry room. I took a deep breath and let it out slowly. I didn't want her to see the stress I was feeling right now.

"Want some help?" I offered.

"Always."

I moved in beside her in front of a stainless-steel laundry table, grabbed a few of the girls' shirts, and began folding. I could never keep straight which clothes belonged to Olivia or Nicole. They were close to the same size.

"Your mom seems to be in better spirits this afternoon."

"It comes in waves. It helps that the girls make her laugh."

"It helps us all. How're you doing?"

Taylor let out a deep sigh. "Up and down. I keep having these fleeting moments where I actually forget my dad is even gone. Like earlier, I was putting the dishes away. The girls were playing a board game with my mom in the living room. And for just a brief moment, I forgot. And I had this fleeting thought, like, I wondered what time my dad was coming over to join us. Then reality hit me again. I suddenly remembered and could barely breathe, it felt so overwhelming."

"It's going to be like that for a while."

"How long? Because I hate the feeling."

"I don't know, babe."

Taylor took a breath and exhaled. "I wish I had one more chance to tell him how much I loved him."

"Your dad knew, Taylor. You made it very clear every day."

"I guess. It's just . . . I want to escape it all. Plus, I'm already tired of people stopping by the house with food and flowers. I know they mean well, but it all feels like too much. I really just want some space to breathe."

"Well, what if right after the funeral on Saturday, we take your mom and the girls out to the lake house for a few days? Might be good for all of us to get away after this tough week. Turn our phones off and just be together. Share stories, drink, laugh."

My in-laws had a beach-style house with a ski boat on the north side of Lake Travis about forty-five minutes away. The girls loved going there on the weekends and being out on the water. Joe and I would usually grill every meal. We'd all sit out on the deck and watch the sun set over the lake. They were really good times.

"I like that idea," Taylor agreed. "I'll run it past my mom."

"Good." I kissed her on the cheek. "Sorry to skip out on the rest of the folding, but I need to finish up some work in my office."

As I began to walk out of the laundry room, Taylor said, "Hey, how did it go with Steve? Mom said you had some questions about the investment money."

I swallowed. For a moment, I didn't respond. I was afraid to tell Taylor the truth because I still didn't know what I was going to discover at the end of all this. The truth felt frightening at the moment. Finding out that Joe had millions basically hidden in a foreign bank account that no one knew about and that he'd lied about his recent trip to DC left me wondering what else he might have misled his family about. I didn't even want to crack open that door with Taylor right now. My wife was hurting. I wanted to protect her and shield her. But I also didn't want to lie to her. We'd made a serious covenant a long time ago to always be honest. Standing there, feeling caught in the crosshairs of her direct question, I thought about how she'd made it so clear to me that she valued truth over everything on the night I'd proposed to her.

We'd had dinner and drinks at Jack Allen's, one of our favorite restaurants, followed by the Broadway show Wicked *at the Bass Concert Hall—Taylor loved musicals—and finally the moment of reckoning. I pulled my Jeep Cherokee into an empty parking lot outside of our old high school track stadium and parked. From the passenger seat, Taylor looked over at me with narrow eyes.*

"Alex? Why are we at our high school?"

"I need you to come with me."

"Come with you where?"

"Just trust me."

I got out of my Jeep, hustled around to open the door for her. She climbed out. Taylor was wearing a simple black cocktail dress and heels and looked more stunning than I could ever remember. I wore a black sport coat with an unbuttoned white dress shirt and jeans. We were more dressed up than usual. Taylor thought it was just for the fun of going to a Broadway show. I had something more in mind. And I could feel my heart rate start picking up the closer I got to popping the life-changing question.

I held out my hand for her. "Let's go."

She hesitantly put her hand in mine. Then I guided her toward a gate in the fence that surrounded the small stadium. The gate was unlocked. People from the community were allowed to access the track for their own exercise throughout the week. But I doubted anyone would be out here tonight. It was late, and the stadium lights were off. I began to lead Taylor toward the bleachers.

"Are we going to make out under the bleachers like we did back in high school?" she asked me with a sideways glance.

I gave her a nervous laugh. "Not yet. Maybe later."

Circling the bleachers, we moved out onto the rubber track. It was dark but not so dark that we couldn't find our way forward. I saw no flashlights circling the track. It looked like we were here alone—except for a friend of mine who was standing near an electrical box, and Taylor's parents, who I knew were hidden behind the bleachers somewhere. The thought of Joe and Carol watching this made me even more nervous. But I wanted them to be here for this moment. Taylor was their only daughter. I just hoped she didn't throw me an unexpected curveball.

Continuing to hold hands, we began walking the track.

"You're acting so weird, Alex," Taylor said. "What's going on?"

"This track is special to me."

"Why? You didn't even run track in school."

"I know. But you did. And I loved watching you run."

"That's sweet. But I still don't get why we're here."

"Because this is where I first fell in love with you six years ago."

She turned. "What? Here?"

I could feel a lump the size of a boulder in my throat. I stopped, pointed down to the track. "This very spot right here."

"Why this spot?"

"Don't you remember? This is where I was when you raced past me and turned back to say, 'Come on, slowpoke' before winning our little contest."

She laughed. "I really kicked your ass that day, didn't I?"

I laughed with her. "Yes, you did."

"You deserved it."

"Most definitely. What I don't deserve is you, Taylor."

She gave me a shy smile. "Stop."

"I mean it," I continued. "But having said that . . ."

With shaky legs, I got down on one knee. When I did, the stadium lights suddenly flashed on all around us. My friend's timing was perfect. Taylor looked around at all the bright lights with wide eyes and then back at me kneeling before her. She put a hand to her mouth, clearly stunned by this moment. We had, of course, casually talked about marrying one day all throughout our dating years. But I had intentionally dodged the topic this last semester of college in an effort to make this a surprise. By the look on her face, I knew I'd pulled it off. Now I just hoped that she didn't surprise me right back.

"Taylor," I began, my voice cracking, "I started loving you in that moment. I have loved you every moment since—imperfectly, at times, I know. And if you'll have me, I want to keep loving you for the rest of my life. Will you marry me?"

I pulled out a ring I'd asked her mother to help me to custom create. I'd saved up for a modest middle diamond surrounded by several other smaller diamonds from her grandmother's wedding ring. I knew she'd appreciate the sentimentality.

For a moment, Taylor just stood there, both hands to her mouth.

"Babe?" I said.

"Of course I'll marry you!"

I sprang to my feet, embraced her.

Then she pulled back. "On one condition."

I cocked my head. "I don't have to race you again, do I?"

She smiled but then wrinkled her forehead. "I'm serious."

"Okay. What condition?"

"No lies, ever. Okay?"

"Of course."

"I mean it, Alex," she said even more sternly. "I can't do this with you unless we're serious about this commitment. If we want to have the kind of relationship my parents have had all these years, we have to make a covenant with each other, right here, right now. Or we can't go forward with this."

"I promise you, Taylor. No lies, ever."

The smile on her face nearly exploded.
"Good. Let's get married!"

I had remained true to that covenant. But this was something entirely different.

"How did it go with Steve?" Taylor repeated. "Is everything good?"

"Yeah, for sure. We're good."

I swallowed again and quickly walked out of the room because I didn't want her to keep pressing me on it. But the lie felt like acid on my tongue.

SIXTEEN

The next morning, I woke really early and asked Taylor if she'd be okay if I put in several hours at the office to catch up on a few important work items. She said it was fine. I kissed her goodbye before she even got out of bed. But I didn't go to the office. Instead, I made the three-hour drive north up I-35 to Dallas. My list of lies was beginning to grow and made me feel so conflicted. But Ethan Tucker clearly knew *something* about Joe's investment money. I wasn't simply going to leave him alone. The man might be able to sidestep my phone calls, but he was going to have a difficult time avoiding me when I showed up to meet with him face-to-face. I really hoped he might give me a sensible explanation for all this. I hated the uneasy feeling stirring inside me that Joe might have been killed for reasons that were connected to the funding for my company.

I arrived a few minutes before ten. Lone Star Financial was on the twelfth floor of a downtown office building near Reunion Tower with its ball-shaped observation deck. I took the elevator up and found myself standing in front of a young receptionist with a nameplate identifying her as Maggie.

She was all grins. "Hi, can I help you?"

"I hope so, Maggie. First, you can tell me where you got those cool earrings. Because my wife would *love* them."

I figured a little charm might help me get in to see Ethan without an appointment.

Her smile grew bigger. "Aw, thanks. I got them over at Aéropostale."

"Perfect. You just made birthday gift buying a little easier for me."

"Glad to hear it. Who are you here to see today?"

"Mr. Ethan Tucker."

The smile on Maggie's face quickly disappeared. "Oh, do you, uh . . . do you have an appointment?"

"Yes," I lied. "Jeff Bagley. Ten o'clock. I'm a few minutes early."

"Uh, okay."

"This was last minute," I explained, noticing a clear change in her affable demeanor. "I scheduled this with him personally yesterday."

"Oh, well, it's just . . . Can you give me just a moment, Mr. Bagley?"

"Certainly."

Maggie left her reception desk with a concerned look on her face and headed around the corner. I wondered why she suddenly seemed frazzled. I went over in my mind what I would say upon seeing Ethan in a few seconds. I knew I'd have to get straight to the point. Once he found out who I really was, he might tell me to get lost again and turn back around. But I was prepared to cause a scene if he refused to answer my questions. I needed to know why talking to me about the investment money was dangerous.

A few seconds later, Maggie returned, along with an older gray-haired man in a blue suit and red tie who was not Ethan Tucker—based on the profile page I'd been looking at on their website yesterday. He came right up to me with a forced smile. "Mr. Bagley, my name is Ted Ashton. I'm the managing partner here at Lone Star Financial."

We shook quick hands.

"Do you mind if I speak to you in private?" Ted asked me.

"About?"

"It will just take a moment. Right over here in our main conference room."

"Okay."

I glanced over at Maggie, who had a bit of deer-in-the-headlights look about her, and then I followed the man into the glass conference room. Again, I wondered what the hell was going on. I was starting to get a bad feeling about showing up here without an appointment. Had Ethan Tucker put out an alert to be on the lookout for any unexpected visitors who might come to see him? That seemed highly unlikely. I wasn't threatening him. Plus, something like that would have probably put me in front of a buff security guard and not the firm's managing partner. So what was the deal? Ted shut the glass door behind us and offered me a seat at the end of an expansive conference table.

I politely declined sitting and asked, "What's going on, Ted?"

"I'm afraid I have difficult news to share and wanted to be as sensitive to the situation as possible. You see, Ethan was tragically killed late last night."

My mouth parted open. "What?"

"It's awful, really. He was shot during an apparent mugging in our parking garage. We're all reeling this morning. His assistant was supposed to cancel all meetings that were on his calendar today. I'm very sorry you were not contacted. Please accept my sincerest apologies."

"No, it's . . . fine." My head was starting to spin. "A mugging?"

"Yes. Building security says there's video of it. But police haven't caught the guy yet, so it's got us all on pins and needles."

I was stunned. Ethan Tucker had been shot dead just hours after saying it was too dangerous to talk to me about Joe. That was not a coincidence.

"Did you have a long-standing relationship with Ethan?" Ted asked me.

"No, we actually only spoke on the phone one time."

"Well, if our firm can still help you, please let us know. Again, I apologize that you came here only to receive this kind of terrible news."

Before stepping back into the elevator, I returned to the receptionist. Maggie looked guilty about our exchange a few minutes ago. "I'm sorry about acting so weird earlier. I didn't know what I was supposed to say when you showed up and asked for Mr. Tucker. It caught me off guard."

"I completely understand. Did you know him well?"

"Not really. I just started here a couple of months ago."

"Me, neither. But I'd still like to send flowers over to his house. Can you possibly get me his home address?"

"Of course." She typed on her computer, scribbled down an address on her notepad, and then handed it to me. "That's real nice of you."

"It's the least I can do. Can you remind me of his wife's name?"

She again looked at her computer. "Sheila."

"Thanks. One more quick thing, Maggie, if you don't mind. Part of why I was here to see Ethan today was to talk about my father-in-law's financial situation. I was wondering if you could tell me how long Joe Dobson has been a client of this firm?"

She typed in her computer and squinted at her screen. "Dobson?"

"Yes." I spelled out the last name.

"Sorry. I don't see his name on our client list."

"Okay, maybe I was wrong. Thanks for checking."

As I got into the elevator, I pulled out my phone and again brought up Ethan Tucker's profile page on the firm's website. His professional bio said he'd been with Lone Star Financial for more than a decade. If Joe was not an official client of the firm, how did they know each other? Why was Ethan the one to wire the $5 million to my father-in-law three years ago? I had another stop to make before going home.

SEVENTEEN

I drove straight to Ethan Tucker's home. He lived in a massive redbrick Colonial in an affluent neighborhood called University Park. Several cars were parked out front in a bush-lined circular driveway. I felt uneasy about knocking on the door of this home the morning after the man had died. His wife and family would be in a state of disbelief and grief that I knew too well. But Joe had said Ethan was an old friend. I had to see if Sheila Tucker also knew my father-in-law and could provide me with some insight. Holding a vase of flowers that I'd picked up on the way over, I stepped up to the front door, knocked, and shifted my weight back and forth while trying to figure out exactly how to approach this. I wanted to be sensitive to their situation.

A large man, probably in his midfifties, with a brown beard, answered the door wearing tan slacks and a black polo shirt. "Yes?"

"Good morning. My name is Alex Mahan," I explained. "I'm sorry for just showing up here on a day like today. But I was wondering if I could have a few minutes to speak with Mrs. Tucker. Her husband was friends with my father-in-law, who was also tragically killed just this past week."

I thought maybe the shared shock and grief over the recent death of a loved one might help get me a moment with Ethan's wife. But it didn't seem to work.

He frowned at me. "My sister is exhausted. Can you come back later?"

"I promise I'll be *very* brief."

"Look, tomorrow would be better, okay?"

Damn. He wasn't budging. "I understand. It's just . . . I live in Austin. I'm only here for the day."

Then I heard a female voice in the hallway behind the large man. "Todd, let him in."

He turned while keeping the door mostly closed. "You need to go rest, Sheila. You don't need people showing up here all day long."

"Don't tell me what I need or don't need. This is still my house."

Sheila Tucker shooed her brother away and was standing at the door in front of me a second later. She had brown hair pulled back into a tight ponytail and wore a burgundy jogging outfit. Her face was red and puffy with little makeup, and her whole body kind of sagged. I'd seen the same hollowed-out eyes in my mother-in-law the past few days.

"You'll have to forgive my brother. He's being overly protective today."

"As he should be, Mrs. Tucker. My deepest condolences."

"Tell me your name again."

"Alex Mahan. These are for you."

She took the flowers. "Thank you. Please, come inside."

She opened the door and allowed me into the spacious foyer. A grand winding staircase was off to my left. A study was to my immediate right. The inside of the house was even more impressive than the outside. The Tuckers had done very well for themselves. She set the vase of flowers on a long entry table that already held several other flower ensembles.

"Did I hear you say your father-in-law was recently killed?"

"Yes, ma'am. Just last week. We were on a trip to Mexico as a family when he was abducted and then later killed by local criminals."

Sheila put her hand to her mouth. "Oh my . . . that's terrible, Alex. I'm so sorry. Why are there such evil people in this world?"

"I don't know. But we're both experiencing the worst of it right now."

"Yes, we are. I just . . . I can't believe it. I don't want to believe it."

"I'm very sorry for your sudden loss, Mrs. Tucker."

She dabbed her eyes with a wadded tissue she already had clutched in her right hand. "You said your father-in-law was friends with Ethan?"

"Yes, Joe Dobson. Did you know him?"

She shook her head. "No, I didn't. How were they friends?"

"I'm honestly not sure. I actually drove up to Dallas from Austin today to see your husband about it when they told me the tragic news over at his office. That's why I came here. Please forgive me for showing up uninvited. I didn't know what else to do. I'm trying to sort out financial matters for my mother-in-law, who is grieving like you, and part of that involves figuring out if Joe and Ethan worked together on the startup funding for my company."

"I'm sorry, Alex, I don't know much about Ethan's work. And I don't recall him ever mentioning the name Joe Dobson."

I pulled out my phone and showed her a photo. "This is Joe."

"He doesn't look familiar to me."

"Did you ever hear Ethan talk about Illuminate? That's the name of my company."

Another shake of the head. "No, sorry."

Someone hollered after Sheila from another room.

"Will you excuse me for just a moment?" she said to me.

"Of course."

She disappeared down a long hallway. My shoulders dropped. So much for finding the connection between Joe and Ethan. What the hell should I do now? I took a few steps into the study. A wall of floor-to-ceiling mahogany shelves sat behind a large antique wooden desk. Two brown leather chairs were in front of the desk. The whole room dripped with rich luxury. I presumed this was Ethan's home office. There was a laptop sitting on top of the desk with several stacks of paper next to it. The mahogany shelves were lined with various leather books, mementos, and framed photos. I stepped up closer to the shelves and began examining the pictures. There were dozens of Ethan with what looked like his family. Kids and grandkids at various stages of life. My heart hurt for this family who, like us, had just had their patriarch stolen from them.

I made my way across the mahogany shelves, getting a real feel for the life of Ethan Tucker, and then paused when I noticed a small framed photo of a college golf team. I leaned in closer. SMU Golf. Thirty-eight years ago. Twelve college-age young men stood side by side dressed in old-fashioned golf attire of red, blue, and white. Their names were listed on the bottom of the photo. I quickly found the name *Ethan Tucker* and spotted him in the photo. Then my eyes drifted two guys over to the left from him and suddenly locked in on another face. I recognized it immediately. My father-in-law. He was young, but it was definitely him. I knew those eyes so well. My face bunched up. That didn't make sense. Joe did not go to SMU. He went to the University of North Texas.

I searched the names at the bottom of the team photo again. Joe's name was not listed anywhere. Instead, in the spot where he stood, it said *Daniel Gibson*. What the hell? I looked back and forth several times. I was certain this was my father-in-law in the golf team photo. Daniel Gibson? I suddenly flashed on the old legal boxes I'd found in Joe's storage unit belonging to Bruce Gibson and Daniel Gibson, Attorneys-at-Law. Then I thought about the letter from Greta I'd discovered in the back of one of those boxes. The envelope had been addressed to Joe, but the letter was actually written to Daniel. My eyes went back to the golf photo and narrowed on my father-in-law.

Could Joe and Daniel be one and the same?

My thoughts were interrupted by Sheila, who stood at the door to the study. "Ethan was an All-American golfer at SMU."

I quickly put the golf-team photo back on the shelf. "I apologize, Mrs. Tucker. I just drifted in here while I was waiting."

"It's okay."

"Do you happen to know someone named Daniel Gibson?"

"No, I don't recognize that name, either."

I motioned toward the framed photo. "He was on the golf team with your husband. I think he might have also been connected with Joe, my father-in-law."

I didn't reveal anything further. Sheila had more than enough to deal with right now without being pulled deeper into this mystery. At least, not yet.

"Ethan and I didn't meet until well after college. I don't think he kept up with too many people from those days. I'm sorry I'm not much help to you."

"No need to be sorry. I've taken up enough of your time."

I again offered Sheila my heartfelt sympathies. Before leaving, I took out a business card from my wallet. "Mrs. Tucker, if you happen to come across anything related to Joe Dobson, would you mind giving me a call? I would really appreciate it."

"Certainly."

I hustled up the street, jumped into my Tahoe, and immediately began searching Google on my phone for the name *Daniel Gibson*. There were *a lot* of mentions of that name online. Musicians, athletes, random other characters. I searched through several online pages with results that took me all over the place. Unfortunately, none of them looked even remotely related to my father-in-law. I did another search: *Bruce Gibson and Daniel Gibson, Attorneys-At-Law*. Nothing at all came up online about the lawyers. I was not surprised. The boxes of legal files in the storage unit were from thirty-five years ago. A third Google search: *Daniel Gibson, SMU.* I squinted at my phone screen. I got a few hits with this one, just old college golf tournament results and golf stats on a couple of obscure sports websites. No photos or write-ups about Daniel Gibson. That wasn't much help other than confirming that someone named Daniel Gibson did indeed play golf at SMU a long time ago. I did a final search: *Joe Dobson, Daniel Gibson.* Nothing grouping the two names together pulled up.

Sighing, I leaned back in my car seat. The only thing I had to go on right now was the SMU golf-team photo. Using my Maps app, I located SMU's campus nearby. Perhaps I could find something more about Daniel Gibson in the university's library archives. It was worth a shot. I still had time before I needed to get back on the road to Austin.

I started my vehicle but then sat there a moment. I again thought about the old letter from Greta to Daniel I'd found in the storage unit. Was that really written to Joe? *I will always consider you my husband.* Could Joe have been married before? I searched for the name *Greta Gibson* online and found a few random listings. But none of the women were the age where they looked connected to my father-in-law. The letter had used the phrase *c'est la vie (such is life).* I swallowed, recalling now how Joe had used the same French phrase with me once before, during the reception after my wedding. Was he talking about Greta?

"Have I told you how beautiful you look?" I'd whispered to Taylor.

She grinned. "About a dozen times already."

"Only a dozen? I have some serious catching up to do."

"I won't stop you."

We both smiled. My face actually hurt from smiling so much tonight. Taylor had her arms around my shoulders while we slow danced in the middle of the banquet room, surrounded by two hundred of our closest family and friends. Everyone had been laughing, dancing, eating, and drinking to

95

their hearts' delight as the live band Taylor had handpicked belted out all our favorite songs. I'd never seen Taylor look so happy. She truly glowed in her beautiful white wedding gown.

I whispered into her ear again. "Can't we sneak out of here already?"

She giggled. "Not yet. Be patient."

"That's never been my strong suit."

"We have the entire honeymoon, babe."

"Well, while I know we'll be in beautiful Kauai, I'm not planning on us ever leaving our hotel suite, if you know what I mean."

She shook her head. "You're incorrigible."

"True. And now you're stuck with me."

Taylor's uncle asked if he could step in and dance with the bride. So I gave up my spot in my wife's arms and stole a brief moment for myself off to the side of the banquet room, trying to soak in whatever I could from our big day. The celebration was nothing short of amazing. The best food, the best band, the best venue, the best of everything. My in-laws had clearly spared no expense for their only daughter's special day. All the hard work Taylor and Carol had put in had really paid off. I knew I'd never forget how I felt in this moment. And to think I'd almost blown the whole thing with Taylor six months ago—if not for Joe, my father-in-law. It felt strange but comforting to use that familial term about him now. Joe had certainly been a father figure to me for the past several years. Now we were actual family.

As if on cue, Joe crossed the banquet hall and settled in next to me. He held a glass of red wine in his hand and was smiling ear to ear.

"Look at her," he said, also staring across the floor at Taylor.

"Believe me, I can't stop."

He laughed. "What a party, huh?"

"I can't thank you enough," I told him.

"It's just money, son. I'm fortunate to have it."

"No, I mean for everything you've done for me, Joe. I wouldn't be standing here today if you hadn't given me the little kick I needed."

"You're welcome, son. The joy on my daughter's face right now tells me my gut has been right about you all along."

"I appreciate that."

"So don't blow it," he kidded.

"I don't plan on it."

Then he turned to me, put his hand on my shoulder, pressed his lips together. I could tell Joe was a bit tipsy. "I'm serious, Alex. You're a blessed man. Don't ever forget it. And I'm not just saying this because it's my daughter. I'm saying it because you two are meant to be together. I know the term 'soul mates' gets thrown around casually these days, but I honestly believe in it. That's you and my Taylor. Cherish it. Not everyone gets to end up with their soul mate. Sometimes it tragically slips away. Sometimes one or the other makes a big mistake and lets it go. And, sometimes, it gets brutally stolen from you through very cruel circumstances. That's probably the worst one of all." He took a deep breath and let it out slowly. "C'est la vie."

For a second, my father-in-law's face soured, like someone had pinched two wet fingers around the lit candlewick to his big smile. Momentarily sullen, he stared off, as if thinking about something else. Or someone? I wasn't sure.

"You all right, Joe?"

My father-in-law turned back to me, the smile gradually returning. "You bet. Hey, let's go grab our girls and show everyone here how to properly cut up this dance floor. I didn't get all dressed up for nothing."

I figured that Joe must have been talking about Greta. Had they reconnected recently? Was Greta why Joe was in DC two weeks ago? I again wondered about a possible affair between the two of them. *I think we've been found out.* Could that have somehow played a part in Joe's death?

I put my car into drive, punched the gas, and sped over to the SMU campus.

EIGHTEEN

I paid for parking in a garage and then found my way over to the impressive DeGolyer Library. After roaming for a few minutes among the college students and various sections, I found a helpful library clerk who informed me that most of the university's archives were online and pointed me to a computer station. She suggested I could simply search for what I was looking for rather than starting the tedious task of pulling out old yearbooks and such.

I sat down and typed *Daniel Gibson* into a search box on the computer screen. Forty-nine different results appeared, dating all the way back to 1947. Most were from the *Rotunda*, SMU's student yearbook. I carefully scrolled through them and focused only on the years associated with the dates from the golf-team photo. The first thing that popped up on my screen was the same photo I'd found on Ethan Tucker's shelf. The names on this photo matched Ethan's. The next two listings were for golf-team photos from the two years prior. In each of them, Joe stood among his teammates wearing the official golf-team attire but was again listed as Daniel Gibson. I shook my head and couldn't believe my eyes. What did this all mean? Did my father-in-law change his name after college? If so, why?

A fourth listing pulled up a photo showing my father-in-law in a full-action golf swing at a collegiate tournament. The caption said: *Daniel Gibson places fourth at San Joaquin Country Club in Fresno, California.* A fifth listing in the archive was not golf related. It was a photo of Joe standing with a few other students at a campus event in front of the historic Dallas Hall, which I'd passed on the walk over to the library. They were all wearing jeans and T-shirts. With each discovery, I found myself more baffled. Joe was standing there, smiling away. And yet he was again listed in the caption as *Daniel Gibson.* I scanned the other faces in the photo and then paused on a certain girl two people down from my father-in-law. I immediately recognized her. She was the same attractive blonde woman wearing the red dress in the photo I'd found inside the letter written to Daniel from Greta. I quickly read the other names listed in the caption from the yearbook photo: *Tommy George, Wallace Kaper, Daniel Gibson, Mary Mosely, Greta Varner, and Vanessa Wilkens.*

Greta Varner. I now had a last name.

I pulled out my phone, searched Google for *Greta Varner.* There were only a few listings online. A handful were from obituaries of much older people than the girl in this yearbook photo. There were only two Greta Varners on Facebook, but neither of them looked remotely like the girl in the photo. They couldn't be the same person. I searched for *Greta Varner, DC.* Nothing at all popped up. And that was it. There was *nothing* else online about Greta Varner.

I sat back in my chair, wondered what happened to her. Perhaps she'd gotten married again and changed her last name. I went back to my university archive search. The very next listing I found online felt like it reached out and punched me in my chest so hard, I could barely breathe. It was a *Dallas Times Herald* news article reprinted in an SMU Dedman School of Law publication called *The Brief* from thirty-five years ago.

Father and Son Lawyers Die in Plane Crash

Bruce Gibson and Daniel Gibson tragically died in a small plane crash outside of El Paso on February 23. The father and son lawyers had their own firm, Gibson & Gibson, Attorneys-at-Law. An investigation is ongoing, but local authorities believe the cause of the crash was mechanical failure.

Blake Crosby, a technician at the one-runway airport, said, "The plane took off normally and then just suddenly exploded. Never seen anything like it."

The two attorneys were in El Paso to meet with a client, according to Lorena Myers, a secretary with the two-man law firm. "We're all shocked and heartbroken," Myers said. "Bruce and Daniel were such good people who will be greatly missed."

Bruce Gibson, an avid pilot, had been practicing law for twenty-seven years in the Dallas area. Daniel Gibson graduated fifth in his class last year from SMU Dedman School of Law and chose to join his father in private practice over several offers from top law firms around the country, according to law school dean Martin Becker. "Daniel was a dedicated student with a bright future," Becker said. "The SMU family mourns this loss." Funeral details are still pending.

There was a photo above the news article showing my father-in-law and Bruce Gibson standing together in what must've been their law office at the time. Both men were wearing business suits. I recognized Bruce Gibson because Joe had a photo of his father on the shelf of his home office. But I did not know him as Bruce Gibson. I knew him as Bruce Dobson. I read the article again and had a difficult time processing it. The article said Daniel Gibson died on February 23. I again thought about the letter from Greta to Daniel. I was sure the date written on the letter was March 19 of the same year—more than three weeks *after* his supposed death. What did that mean?

How had my father-in-law once been Daniel Gibson and then switched to being Joe Dobson after he'd supposedly died in a plane crash along with his father? My father-in-law had told me his father had died while Joe was in his twenties. But Joe said it was a car wreck. Not a plane crash. As far as I knew, Joe did not have any other family. He said his mother, who had been estranged from her own family, had passed away from an illness when he was just a toddler. He was an only child. And his father had no brothers or sisters. So Taylor and I never traveled anywhere to see relatives on his side of the family.

But was that the truth?

What the hell was going on here?

My eyes went back to the news article and found the name of the secretary who was quoted. Lorena Myers. I typed her name into Google on my phone, searched, and found a possible candidate on Facebook. She looked to be around the age of someone who could've been a secretary thirty-five years ago, lived in Dallas, and was very active on social media, making several posts a day—including a post about gardening from only twelve minutes ago. I clicked the "Message" button on her page and quickly typed something out for her.

Hi, Lorena, my name is Alex Mahan. Sorry this is so random. I'm looking for information about Bruce Gibson and Daniel Gibson. I read an old news article written about their deaths where a secretary

> with your name was at their law firm way back when.
> Was that you? I think I may be related to them and
> was hoping you might be willing to talk to me. If so,
> please message me back. I'd really appreciate it!

I went back to searching the university archives but could barely focus. How could I after discovering that the man I knew as my father-in-law, mentor, and friend was actually someone else? Did Carol know anything about this? Had Joe also hidden it from her? If so, why? And did any of this have anything to do with the money Joe had invested in my company? I got a new message alert on my phone from Facebook. As I'd hoped, Lorena Myers had responded to my message right away.

> Hi, Alex, I'd be happy to speak with you about
> Bruce and Daniel. I still have such warm memories
> of both of them. Please feel free to give me a call.
> If you're in Dallas, I'd love to meet you.

She'd typed her phone number. I bolted from the library while dialing.

NINETEEN

I pulled up to a luxury one-story condo complex with lush landscaping surrounding multiple walking trails. Lorena Myers had told me over the phone that she'd sold her house and moved into a unit here after her husband passed away two years ago. The condo allowed her the flexibility to travel more frequently to visit her kids and grandkids, who lived in different parts of the country. Lorena was quite the talker. I hoped that might prove to be helpful. I knocked on the door to her unit, and a woman in her late sixties with a gray bob haircut wearing jeans and a red sweatshirt answered right away. A white poodle yapped away at her feet.

"Hi, Alex, come on in," she said, leading me inside.

"I really appreciate this, Lorena. I'm only in Dallas for the day, so it means a lot that you made the time to talk to me."

"Of course. I don't have much going on today anyway. My gardening group got canceled this afternoon. Margie is sick again. Can I offer you some tea? I have a fresh batch of my favorite hibiscus made up."

"Sure. That would be great."

"Please have a seat."

The condo had a small living room off the kitchen. I could see through the patio doors that the building backed up to what looked like a central garden area with fountains and benches. I took a seat on a flowery couch. The poodle had stopped barking but was still sniffing at my shoes. I reached down to pet the dog, and she rolled over for me to scratch her stomach. Lorena returned a few seconds later with two glasses of tea.

"Zoe loves a good belly rub," she said, smiling. She handed me the tea, and I took a quick sip. It was awful, but I made a yum sound and set it on the glass coffee table.

Lorena jumped right in. "I still think about Bruce and Daniel quite often. Such wonderful guys. It was so tragic for me and everyone when they passed."

"How long did you work for them?"

"I was with Bruce for four years when Daniel joined him after graduating from law school. Daniel was so smart and so enjoyable to be around. He just had this magnetic way about him that always made everyone feel better. It was hard to accept that such a promising life had been cut so short."

I wanted to tell her he had actually gone on to live out a life of real impact. "Were there other staff besides you?"

She nodded. "Two law students who clerked when not in class." She wrinkled her forehead. "What were their names again? Linda and . . . Roger? Oh, I just can't place their last names right now. Getting older has really messed with my memory. They were with us for only a brief time before the accident. Of course, the firm closed right after."

"What can you tell me about the day of the accident?"

She pressed her lips together. "Such a sad day. They flew out really early to El Paso. They had a morning meeting with a client. I was in the office all day, catching up on paperwork. I think Linda was there with me, researching a case for Bruce. I got a call midafternoon from someone who worked at the small airport outside of El Paso. I think he said Bruce had written down our office phone number in a log somewhere. The man told me that their plane had exploded almost immediately after taking off. Two men were inside, and neither one had survived."

She put her hand to her chest. "I still feel nearly the same devastation today that I felt in that moment so many years ago."

"It was Bruce's plane?" I asked.

"Yes, he liked to fly. He was flying well before I started working for him. The little plane allowed them to take on clients from around the state. So he and Daniel would fly off to various places a couple of times a month."

"Did they ever say what caused the crash?"

She twisted her mouth up. "I'm not really sure. I think something with the engine catching on fire. After it happened, I was busy trying to do whatever I could to close the firm while helping transition all our clients. I knew Bruce and Daniel would want me to do that. It probably took me a month before I was able to close the doors for good. Such a strange thing to shut down an entire law firm all by myself. But I did my best."

"I assume you went to their funeral services?"

"Of course. They had a joint service. It was so sad. Daniel had just gotten married. A beautiful young lady named Greta. She was clearly devastated."

"Did you keep in touch with Greta?"

"No, she moved away not long after."

"Were there other family members there?"

"That's part of what made it sad. I guess Bruce didn't have much family. His wife had died when Daniel was little, and he never remarried. I think there might've been a long-lost uncle or something. But that was all. It was mostly friends and business associates—which they had plenty of both."

I tried to figure out how to transition from the facts of the plane crash to the revelation that Daniel Gibson seemed to have actually somehow survived. "Did anyone else travel with them to El Paso?"

"No, the plane was only a two-seater. Bruce offered to take me up once, but I declined. I was so scared of flying back then. After the crash, it took me a long time to get back on any airplane. But then my kids got married and moved away. And soon there were grandkids. Nothing like a grandbaby to help you get over your fears. Now I fly all over the place."

If my father-in-law had not been on that two-seater plane with his father upon takeoff, then who had? It felt surreal to even be pondering such possibilities. My pursuit of answers about Joe's money had led me down a twisting rabbit hole I could have never anticipated. I had no idea how I was going to find my way out of it now without continuing to press forward in search of the truth.

"Did you discover anything unusual while you were spending that month trying to close down the firm?" I asked her.

Her brow bunched. "Unusual?"

"About their cases or anything in their files?"

"Not that I recall. Honestly, I didn't spend too much time going through their cases. I was just trying to box everything up appropriately."

"What did you do with the boxes?"

"I stored them in my garage for a while. Wasn't sure if I needed to hold on to them or not. I asked another lawyer friend, and he told me to do that, just in case. After a few years, I had them all shredded. Well, except for two of them."

"What happened to those two?"

"They got stolen from the office. Can you believe that? A few days after the accident, I came into the office late one night because I'd forgotten something at my desk. When I got there, I noticed a light was on in our back conference room. We only had a small office suite with a couple of rooms for Bruce and Daniel and a conference room in the back. I always made it a habit to turn off the lights, so I was surprised to see the glow from the back. When I walked back there to take a look, some guy was climbing out the window to the parking lot. Scared me to death, so I quickly called the police. After reviewing everything, I realized two boxes I'd packed were missing."

"You think the guy stole them?"

"I do. Back then, I was as sharp as a whip. I took tremendous pride in my organizational skills. I had logged each box I was packing away. Two of them on my log were gone. I have no other explanation for it."

"Do you recall what was inside those boxes?"

"I don't remember," she said, shaking her head.

I tossed out one more question. "Lorena, was there anything suspicious about the plane crash?"

"What do you mean?"

"After it happened, were there ever any rumors floating around about other reasons the plane might have crashed besides engine failure? Or if there might have actually been, uh . . . survivors?"

She kind of frowned at me. "No, I never heard such things."

I played it off. "Just curious. Over time, these stories have a way of taking on different forms depending on whom you talk with."

I saw her kind of look off for a moment, as if thinking about something and hesitant to tell me for some reason.

"What is it?" I asked.

She leaned forward in her chair, like she was going to tell me a secret and didn't want anyone else to hear. "Well, I don't know about rumors and all of that. But between you and me—and I didn't even tell the police this the night those boxes were stolen because I knew they'd think I was crazy. But for a brief moment, I could've sworn the guy jumping out of the conference room window and running away was Daniel. I never really saw his face up close, but he wore a black hoodie just like Daniel always used to wear. It was only a split second, and then the guy was out the window and long gone. Probably just my mind's way of processing the grief of it all. But it was so strange."

"You ever tell anyone?"

She shook her head. "No, no, never. Everyone would think I was a kook."

I thought about the two boxes I'd found in storage.

Had my father-in-law gone back to grab them in the middle of the night?

If so, why? Who was the client? And what was valuable in them?

TWENTY

I needed to get back on the road to Austin soon, or I'd be late for dinner. Taylor would surely bust me for being late. She already seemed annoyed that a few hours at the office had turned into something much more extended. I'd made a commitment to her three years ago, when I'd started my company, to always be home to sit at the dinner table with our girls. Other than some travel here and there, I'd rarely broken that commitment. I could certainly offer her no viable excuse for being late today since I was supposedly only a few miles from home all day.

Each time Taylor and I had texted today, I'd felt the guilt building. And I'd just opened the lid to Pandora's box about her father. What the hell was I supposed to do now?

But I had one more stop to make. I'd reached out to an old college pal for a quick meetup before jumping back on I-35. Brian Jones used to play linebacker on the football team with me. He then spent three years bouncing around the NFL before pursuing law enforcement. His father had been a cop in Shreveport for forty years. His grandfather before that. Brian had recently been promoted to Dallas PD detective. We still regularly kept up with each other. I pulled up to Lee Harvey's, a dive bar with a fenced-in gravel patio, and found Brian waiting for me out front. Wearing a blue button-down with the sleeves rolled up and gray slacks, my friend still looked very much like the hulking line-backer from his playing days. Although he now shaved his brown head completely bald, and it shone in the afternoon sunlight.

We shared a quick handshake and a bro hug.

"You look like hell, Mahan," he said to me.

"Been a rough week. Not getting much sleep."

"Man, I'm sorry to hear about Taylor's dad. You doing all right?"

I wasn't sure how to answer that right now. "I'm making it. Trying to be strong for all of my girls, you know?"

"I hear ya. You want a beer? I'm off duty."

"Nah, I better not. I've got to hit the road. Were you able to get it?"

He nodded, pulled out his phone. "What's this all about?"

I'd asked Brian if he could get the building security footage from the parking garage where Ethan Tucker had been killed last night. The managing partner at Ethan's firm had mentioned it earlier.

"I just need to see it. I can't really tell you much more right now. You'll have to trust me. I came up here this morning to talk to this guy about some financial matters only to find out about what happened last night. You watch it?"

"Yeah. Looks pretty straightforward to me. Guy walks up to him, they struggle, he gets shot. You sure you want to see a guy get killed?"

"I do."

"All righty."

Brian pressed a few things on his phone screen, brought up a video, and then handed it over to me. I held it close to my face. The security camera looked like it was installed in a corner near the garage's elevator. The time stamp on the video said it was 11:17 p.m. A man in a dark suit with gray hair holding a black briefcase appeared in camera view, probably from out of the elevator. Although I couldn't see his face, I presumed it was Ethan Tucker. He paused, stuck his hand inside his suit jacket, pulled out a key fob, and then aimed it and pressed a button. A white car in the distance blinked its lights. It looked like it might be a

BMW sedan. The garage level was nearly empty. Only a few random vehicles here and there.

Ethan had taken a step toward the car when another man suddenly appeared from off-screen and stepped right in front of him. It was a side shot of the guy, so I caught only a small glimpse of his face. He wore a black jacket and black pants. A brief but animated conversation ensued between the two men. There was no sound on the footage. When Ethan tried to step around him, the guy pulled a gun out of his jacket. Instead of dropping his briefcase and holding his hands up, like any normal person would do, Ethan lunged for the gun. They had a very brief struggle, and then Ethan kind of jerked, dropped to his knees, and clutched his hands to his chest. The other guy seemed to be yelling at him. But Ethan didn't respond. A second later, Ethan fell forward onto his side and lay perfectly still. The guy in black knelt over him, began searching his pockets, and found what looked like his wallet inside his suit jacket.

At that moment, the guy turned fully toward the camera, almost as if he were looking to see if there was a security camera. Then he got up and ran out of view. I quickly rewound it and paused it when the guy was staring directly at the camera. Then I cursed, felt a ripple of terror push through me. It was the intruder who'd assaulted me the other night. The same Mexican guy who had stood in the village crowd the day Joe had been abducted. I felt my pulse immediately quicken.

"Everything all right, man?" Brian asked me. "You look a bit rattled."

I wasn't sure what to tell my old friend. It couldn't be the truth. He might tell his wife, who was college friends with Taylor. I had to keep any of this from getting back to Taylor until I had more time to figure out what was going on. "Yeah, I just had to see it for myself. Hard to believe. Do y'all have any leads on this guy?"

"It's not my case, but I don't believe so. Not yet."

Brian excused himself to go to the restroom inside the bar and left his phone with me to watch the video again. I took out my own phone and quickly snapped a closeup photo of the face of the Mexican guy staring up at the security camera.

After saying goodbye to Brian, I sat in my Tahoe for a moment, my heart racing, and sent a text that included the photo of Ethan's killer to Raul.

Call me as soon as you get this.

My phone rang within seconds.

I went straight into it. "This is the guy, Raul. The one from the village that day who was inside Joe's house with me the other night. Do you recognize him?"

"No, I don't. Where did you get the photo?"

"A detective friend here in the States."

"It looks like a still from security-camera footage."

"It is. The guy killed a man in a parking garage in Dallas late last night. A man I had just spoken to about Joe's death on the phone yesterday." I quickly explained my phone call with Ethan Tucker and how I'd come to Dallas this morning to meet with him in person. "I need you to help me find the identity of this guy. It all has to be connected to Joe's kidnapping and death."

"I'll work on it. Do you think you're in danger, amigo?"

"Maybe. I don't know."

"Well, be safe. I'll get back to you as soon as I have something."

Hanging up my phone, I started my Tahoe and then paused to wait for another vehicle to pass by me from the opposite direction before entering the street. A gray Ford Taurus. I glanced at the driver, who was staring right back at me. Then I tried to do a quick double take, but the Taurus was already in my rearview mirror and turning a corner. I could've sworn the driver was the same fiftysomething mustached bald guy with the navy tattoo whom I'd bumped into by the elevator yesterday.

TWENTY-ONE

I barely made it home in time for dinner. At the last minute, Taylor called and asked me to stop off at the grocery store when leaving the office to pick up a few things. My wife had made one of my favorite meals—an enchilada casserole, tamales, and a salad—which made me feel even worse about all the lying. I took the deepest breath possible and let it out slowly before I stepped inside the house from the garage. I was about to have to do the best bluffing of my life, even though I felt like I was wearing the shock of the day all over my face. I walked into the kitchen, set two sacks of groceries on the counter, and made my way over to Taylor, who was mixing the salad. We shared a quick kiss. Thankfully, she didn't seem too irritated about my absence all day.

"How's it going around here?" I asked.

My voice kind of cracked; I was already blowing it.

"Well, Olivia just got angry and threw a Barbie at Nicole, who wasn't sharing doll clothes, and it bopped her good on the head. I think she'll have a bump. That, of course, brought on about a half hour of emotional hysterics. So that's where things currently stand."

"So the usual?"

This brought a small smile to my wife's lips. "Right."

"Where are they?"

"My mom is getting them bathed in our bathroom."

I could hear laughter coming from the back of the house. "Sounds like all is good now."

"My mom probably bribed them with candy. She's been giving them whatever they want the past two days."

"She just wants to see them happy. The girls will survive."

"I know. I just . . . I want things to go back to normal."

"We'll have to figure out a new normal."

Taylor went over to check on the casserole. "How's everything at the office?"

I swallowed. "Good. Thanks again for letting me get some work done."

"I have to admit, I'm jealous. I'd love to be able to escape into my work for a little while and not have to live in this hard stuff every moment of the day. But that feels impossible with my mom here all the time."

"Maybe it'll get easier after the service."

"I hope so. Speaking of that, how're you doing with the photo presentation?"

I swallowed again. I hadn't even started it. "Making progress."

"Can I see what you have so far?"

"Uh, not yet . . . let me keep polishing it up."

The girls both came out of the back hallway wearing their pajamas with wet hair, yelled "Daddy!" with delight, and raced toward me. This was pretty much the highlight of my every day. I scooped up Olivia with my right arm and Nicole with my left and hugged them both really tight. I took a glance at Nicole's forehead, where she definitely had a little bump near her hairline.

"That's a nice bruise on your head," I said to Nicole.

"Sissy got mad at me," Nicole replied.

I gave a stern look to Olivia.

She frowned. "I already said I was sorry, Daddy."

"What do we say about hitting, kicking, or throwing things at each other?"

"I know," Olivia said, hanging her head.

"It's okay, Daddy," Nicole chimed in. "Sissy gave me Courtney to play with to make up for it."

"Only for *one* day," Olivia quickly corrected.

I smiled at Olivia. Courtney was her favorite American Girl doll. My seven-year-old must've really felt bad about the bump on her sister's head.

"Grab your seats, girls," Taylor said, removing the casserole dish from the oven and setting it in the middle of our kitchen table.

Carol joined us from the hallway. The sight of her brought a fresh rush of heavy emotions. I again wondered what all she knew about Joe's past. Had he kept everything hidden from her? Or had he let her in on his secret? I couldn't imagine keeping something like this from Taylor. Just carrying around the lies from the past two days was eating me up inside. Had Joe done that for his entire marriage? When the moment was right, I hoped to probe a little with my mother-in-law. But I certainly didn't want to do it in front of Taylor.

I walked over, gave my mother-in-law a quick hug. "How're you doing?"

"Better. Thanks to these two cuties."

She smiled at the girls. I wondered if Carol was going to need to stay with us long-term to make it through this transition without Joe. I was fine with that, but it might drive Taylor crazy. The girls needed boundaries, and my in-laws had never been good at reinforcing them. Every time we dropped them off for a date night, Taylor asked her parents to keep the treats to a minimum. Every time we picked them up, we found out they'd had cookies, ice cream, *and* candy.

We sat around the dinner table and held hands while I quickly blessed the food. Then we loaded up our plates. I immediately began asking the girls a lot of questions about their day, and they gladly told me as many stories as they could think of in the greatest detail. Part of my engagement with them was a tactic to keep the conversation off me and my day. I didn't want to have to bluff my way through dinner.

While listening to one of Nicole's stories about a baby doll, I glanced over to an empty chair at the opposite end of the table where Joe would normally sit. My heart sank. Taylor had set a plate out for him. Probably out of habit. But still, it stung like hell.

For a brief moment, I felt angry at Joe.

Why so many lies?

Did you do something that got you killed?

Are you to blame for all this pain my family is dealing with right now?

After dinner, Carol insisted that she clean the table and do the dishes while Taylor took the girls upstairs to begin bedtime—a routine that could take more than an hour depending on how many times the girls kept getting up. *I need water. I need to go to the bathroom. There's something in my room. Olivia won't stop talking. Nicole won't stop talking.* Both of my girls could go on forever. Fortunately, when they were both finally asleep, they usually stayed down most of the night. It was just *a lot* of work to get them there.

I told Taylor I'd help clean up the kitchen and then join her upstairs in a few minutes. Double-teaming story time was the only chance we had at wrapping things up more quickly. Especially because Olivia and Nicole could never agree on which book they wanted read to them. I grabbed the dirty utensils from the kitchen table and set them in the sink while Carol loaded the dishwasher. I wondered how best to get into this conversation with my mother-in-law.

"Hey, Carol, can you remind me how you met Joe? I was trying to remember earlier today but was murky on the details."

She paused while wiping down a plate, looked up at me, and actually smiled. "I was one of his first clients after he'd moved to Vancouver and opened his law practice."

"That's right. Why did you need a lawyer again?"

"I was waitressing at this little café not far from where he'd rented an office. We had an instant connection. He came in every day for about a week and made sure to always sit in my section. I kept thinking he was going to ask me out, but he took his sweet time. Well, I got fired from that café because the owner got handsy with me, and I wouldn't put up with him. Then he stiffed me my final paycheck. I guess Joe got word of what happened, tracked me down through another waitress, and knocked on my door. I lived in this really dumpy garage apartment. I was so embarrassed. I was dirt poor back then. My father had left when I was just a kid, and my mom struggled with alcohol while I was growing up. I'd basically been on my own since I was sixteen, barely able to make ends meet. Joe was my knight in shining armor. He offered to help me legally with getting me my final paycheck and possibly even more. When he was done threatening legal action with the café owner, I had more than six months' worth of pay to carry me through for a while. But I never needed it. Joe and I fell for each other and quickly got married."

"That must've been a whirlwind."

She smiled again. "Those early years were definitely a wonderful whirlwind. Joe was so charming and such a free spirit. We moved around a lot the first couple of years. We went all over, never staying in one place for very long. Joe only wanted to rent for a while so we were never too tied down." She kind of chuckled. "We even moved overnight one time."

This caught my interest. "Why?"

"Joe came home one day and just said it was time to go. He told me he found this cute little place to rent in a town about two hours away. He really wanted it. But we had to go the very next morning, or we'd probably lose it."

"Why the rush?"

"I don't know. He was just urgent about it. We spent all night packing up our things and were on the road by sunup the next day. It was crazy back then but exciting. There was always something new around the corner. But then two things happened around the same time that made us settle down. I got pregnant with Taylor. And my mom, who had come down to Texas with her loser boyfriend, got really sick. We made the move here so I could care for my mom. Joe didn't really want to move back to Texas, but he did it for me. My mom probably lived several more years than she would have without me here with her. So I felt blessed by that."

I decided to probe more aggressively. I didn't have all night to dance around this. I knew Taylor would be hollering down for me shortly.

"Carol, when y'all were in Canada, did you know a guy named Daniel Gibson?"

I watched her very closely to see if there was any hint of recognition. Had Joe told her about his other life? But Carol didn't flinch. "No, that name doesn't sound familiar."

Joe had kept that secret from Carol for more than thirty years. Why? It seemed cruel to me. But did my father-in-law have a good reason?

"What about someone named Greta Varner?"

This time I got a definitive response. A quick flash of her eyes that let me know Carol recognized the name. "I haven't heard that name in a *long* time."

"Who is she?"

Carol sighed, took a glance down the hallway toward the stairs, as if she was making sure no one else could hear our conversation. "Just someone from Joe's past."

"Carol?"

"Greta was Joe's first wife."

I tried to feign surprise, even though I'd already made this discovery. "Joe was married before you?"

Carol nodded. "Just briefly."

"Did you know that before you got married?"

She shook her head. "No, I found out a few years later. I was cleaning out his dresser one day when he was at the office, and I found a wedding band in a small jewelry bag with a date engraved inside. When I confronted him, he admitted it was his and said it was all a big mistake. And he was too ashamed to tell me about it."

So Carol was not completely in the dark. But she didn't seem to know that Joe was married to Greta under the name Daniel Gibson.

"Did you ever meet her?" I asked.

"No. Joe never brought her up again. He said he didn't even know where she was. I was curious, of course. But back then, you couldn't simply jump on the internet and search for someone. So this is the first time I've heard her name since that day. How did you find out about her?"

"She was listed in one of Joe's old financial papers," I lied.

"Does Taylor know about Greta?" Carol whispered.

I shook my head. "No, I just came upon the name today."

"Please don't tell her, Alex. I don't want her to think any less of her father."

"People get divorced, Carol. It's not a scarlet letter."

"I know. But if she finds out now, after all this time, she'll probably wonder why her father never told her in the first place. For some reason, Joe just didn't want her to know about his first marriage. And I don't want her thinking he wasn't always honest with her. Honesty was a really big deal between them. Okay?"

"Okay. I'll keep it to myself."

"Thank you."

I wanted to say, *But he wasn't always honest—with any of us. To lengths none of us could possibly fathom.* Instead, I kept my mouth shut. But I could see now how family lies could spread like a destructive virus through generations. Which made my current position with Taylor feel even more excruciating.

TWENTY-TWO

After getting the girls down for bed, I told Taylor I was going over to her parents' house to grab a few framed photos to use in the presentation. Instead, I drove straight to the storage facility where my father-in-law kept his old boxes of legal files. I pressed in the code at the security gate and then parked in a spot outside of the two-story building. It was after dark, and the parking lot was empty. I pressed more codes at the building door to get inside, took the stairs up to the second level, and once again found myself standing in front of the various stacks of boxes. I knew right where to search this time.

I found the two boxes labeled *Bruce Gibson & Daniel Gibson, Attorneys-at-Law*, and popped open the lids on both. First, I searched for the thirty-five-year-old letter from Greta in the back of the second box. I read it again and stuck it in my pocket. Then I began pulling out the files from the boxes. They were all from the same client: Grande Distributors. I found a file labeled *Company Info* and discovered that Grande Distributors had been based out of Mexico City with a distribution center in El Paso. The company mostly stored and transported appliances and electronics to and from Mexico. I did a quick Google search on my phone. The company still existed all these years later and appeared to have grown massive in size and in scope.

I looked deeper into the files. From what I could tell, Joe and his father had represented the company on about a dozen general-litigation matters over about a year's worth of time—so not long. Mostly disputes with truck drivers and issues with wholesalers and vendors. I pored over every word in these files, wondering if one of them could've entailed the mysterious multimillion-dollar settlement. I had skimmed them during my previous visit to the storage unit because they didn't have Joe's name on them. I reached the last file in the second box and found nothing related to a big settlement, nothing unusual at all about the files. So why had Joe secretly taken them from his old office after his supposed death thirty-five years ago?

I packed up the two boxes and put them back with the stacks of others. Then I closed the garage door to the unit and hit the stairs again. Inside the stairwell, I paused and stared out a window to the outside parking lot where I could see my Tahoe parked in its spot. I noticed that a black Ford Explorer was now parked across the parking lot. It had not been there when I'd entered the building. That didn't necessarily concern me. Renters could come and go whenever they pleased. What did concern me was that I could see someone sitting in the shadows of the vehicle behind the steering wheel. The glow of a phone screen cast a slight bit of light on the driver's face. But it wasn't enough to tell anything about the driver. Plus, the driver wore a cap with the bill pulled down low.

Why was someone just sitting there? A passenger could be inside the storage building, and the driver was simply waiting on them. But then why park away from the building instead of up close like me? I was understandably feeling more paranoid since my meeting with Brian in Dallas and knowing I had stood face-to-face with a killer while inside my in-laws' house the other night. I watched for another minute or so, waiting for movement of some kind—either the driver finally leaving, or someone coming out of the building and jumping in the passenger seat. But neither happened. I left my spot near the window and continued to descend to the ground floor. Then I pushed through the door to the parking lot. As I circled my Tahoe, I cast another quick glance toward the Explorer. But it was too difficult to tell if I was being watched.

Climbing behind the wheel, I started up my car and quickly backed out. Then I headed for the exit to the property. I paused as the automatic gate began to open, watching my rearview mirror the entire time, and slowly eased through the gate and up to the street. Just as I pulled into slight traffic, I noticed the headlights of the Explorer pop on behind me in the parking lot.

TWENTY-THREE

I kept my eyes on my rearview mirror. I couldn't tell if the black Ford Explorer was following me. There were too many headlights behind me to make out anything. I sighed, shook my head, tried to convince myself I was being silly. Still, I kept my eyes on my mirrors. A couple of minutes later, I parked in my in-laws' driveway. I wasn't completely lying to Taylor about tonight. I still had intentions of going by my in-laws'—just not to look for framed photos. Instead, I planned to search every nook and cranny of Joe's home office to see if I could find *anything* related to what I'd uncovered over the past twenty-four hours. Entering through the garage, I felt relieved when I heard the alarm beeping and waiting to be disarmed. I didn't want to run into another intruder tonight. From a front window, I peeked out at the street. I didn't spot the Explorer anywhere.

I headed straight to Joe's home office and flipped on the lights. I started with a small closet that held a few legal boxes and a couple of plastic tubs. I pulled out the boxes. Like those in the storage unit, these were also labeled on the outside with black marker for certain clients. Joe still took on a case here and there when he felt like it. I pulled out each and every file and carefully reviewed the paperwork inside to make sure I didn't miss anything. Nothing from the three boxes captured my attention.

The plastic tubs held only miscellaneous office supplies like copy paper, pens, notepads, paper clips, and such. The tubs were probably what my father-in-law used when he'd cleaned out his work office for the last time a few years ago. I had already looked through the three drawers of files that were built into the wall of wood shelves behind Joe's desk. But I wanted to check them again to see if I'd missed anything. I pulled out every file and spread them on the hardwood floor. Nothing peculiar jumped out at me.

Shifting my attention to Joe's desk, I began pulling out drawers and sifting through the contents. The center drawer contained pens, pencils, markers, and various business cards that Joe had collected over the years. I reviewed each of the business cards and then put them back. The next drawer only housed mailing envelopes and labels. A third drawer contained a pile of old bills. The fourth drawer was stuffed full with probably every single handwritten card my daughters had ever given to my father-in-law. This made me pause a moment. I felt a catch in my throat and a sudden flood of grief for my daughters. There would be no more cards made for Papa. My girls had found such joy in creating them. Especially because Joe would go over the top in showing his appreciation for each and every one. I took a deep breath and let it out slowly.

I found something interesting in the bottom left drawer. A small black safe about the size of a shoebox with a small silver logo on it that said *TurboVault*. I pulled the safe out of the drawer and set it on the desk. There was a silver keypad on the front of the box along with a round silver handle. I tried to turn the handle, but it was locked. I had no clue what Joe might have used for the code. I typed in the code for the garage and a light next to the keypad blinked red. Then I typed in the original code for the house alarm. The light again blinked red. Damn. My eyes drifted back over to the name of the TurboVault logo, which looked familiar to me. Did Joe have a TurboVault app on his phone?

Leaving the office, I made my way back out to the driveway and retrieved Joe's cell phone from the center console. I'd been keeping it with me in case anything turned up where I might need something from it. I typed in the security code to access the phone, began scrolling through several pages of apps. Bingo. I found an app for TurboVault on the third page. I returned to the office, opened the app for the safe, and then found an "Unlock" option. I pressed the button on the app, and a green light blinked on the safe.

Inside, I discovered passports for Joe and Carol, official birth certificates for both of them, some jewelry—a diamond necklace, two diamond rings. I knew one of the rings was Taylor's grandmother's wedding ring because I'd used several of the diamonds from it for Taylor's ring. There was also a white envelope with about a thousand dollars' worth of cash inside of it. The final item in the safe was a small black banker's bag.

I quickly unzipped the bag. My eyes widened. Inside, I found a collection of my father-in-law's old IDs, all of them from his twenties. Passport. Driver's license. Student IDs. Gym IDs. None of them identified him as Joe Dobson. They all said Daniel Gibson. Even though I'd been processing this all afternoon, seeing these items up close took my breath away. This was all real and so damn hard to believe. I also found a few IDs for his father, Bruce Gibson. And then I took out several small photographs. Most of them were of Greta, the mystery woman. Several were of both my father-in-law and Greta together. One of the photos I found particularly curious. Greta was standing inside a big building, wearing black capri pants and a gray SMU sweatshirt with a brown backpack over both shoulders. But it was the huge emblem on the glossy floor beneath her that really caught my attention: *Central Intelligence Agency, United States of America.* CIA? Was Greta standing inside a Langley building here? Was she taking some kind of fun college tour? Or could Joe's ex-wife have actually been CIA? I flipped it over but found nothing written on the back.

In the very back of the bag, I found a folded-up old newspaper clipping and unraveled it. *El Paso Times.* I noted the date was from two weeks *after* Daniel Gibson and his father had both died in the plane crash. The article's headline: Prominent Businessman Found Dead.

The article talked about how businessman Eduardo Cortez, founder of a Mexico City–based company called Grande Distributors, had been found dead inside his car just a few miles inside the US border. The scene was gruesome because Cortez had been beheaded. Police were investigating. The article went on to talk about how Cortez was well known around El Paso because his successful company had a local office with several warehouses that employed dozens of people.

Eduardo Cortez and his company were part of the two boxes of legal files Joe had stored away all these years. Why had my father-in-law kept this newspaper article? Was the businessman's death related to the plane crash, and was this why Joe had changed his identity and disappeared? Was this somehow connected with what had just happened to my father-in-law in Matamoros and with Ethan Tucker in Dallas?

A familiar but unexpected voice from the office doorway shook me.

"What are you doing?"

I looked up, found Taylor standing there with her face bunched up. I had been so focused on this new material that I hadn't even heard her enter the house. I felt a sudden panic inside. The banker's bag was open right in front of me, the newspaper clipping still in my fingers. How would I explain any of this to her?

"Hey," I replied, my voice unsteady. "What . . . what are you doing here?"

"Well, with my mom at the house, I thought I'd come over to see if I could help you. Why're you in here? The office is a wreck. What's going on?"

Again, I felt the panic surging. How was I going to get out of this? There was no way I wanted to tell Taylor about any of this right now. Not with her father's funeral service only two days away. I wanted to at least get her past that difficult event before unloading all this onto her. Plus, I was still holding on to hope that I'd find something to make sense of all this craziness and somehow exonerate her father's actions. Opening the door on this tonight meant pulling her into a dark world where her hero father looked very much like a liar and a fraud who might have even been having an affair with his ex-wife. The thought of telling my wife all this ripped at my heart.

I steadied my voice. "I, uh . . . I got an email tonight from Craig Kinney, your dad's financial adviser. He wanted to know if I had come across some passwords on a couple of your dad's financial accounts. I told him I'd see what I could find."

"So you tore apart my dad's office?"

I felt her eyes boring into me. She was suspicious. This was all about to come undone on me if I didn't put on a good show for her right now. "Well, once I got started in here, I couldn't stop myself. I got all emotional looking through your dad's stuff." I thought of a distraction. "Take a look at this, babe."

I pulled out the drawer with all the homemade cards Olivia and Nicole had made for Joe over the past seven years and set it on top of the desk. She walked over and began examining them. As I'd hoped, the sight of the cards from the girls immediately swept her attention away from me. I took that moment to discreetly return everything I'd discovered inside the banker's bag without drawing her attention. And then—making like I was tidying up the desktop—I casually placed the banker's bag in the center drawer and closed it shut, hoping Taylor would never even ask me about it.

"Wow," she said. "He kept them all."

"Of course he did. He cherished every one of them."

"This was one of my favorites," she said, holding up a card Olivia had created for him when she was only four. It had pink-and-purple stick figures with her Papa throwing her into the air with hearts all around it.

"Mine, too."

And off we went looking through each of the homemade cards together.

I slowly exhaled. I had dodged a serious bullet.

But I knew I couldn't keep doing this much longer.

TWENTY-FOUR

I stared at the bedroom ceiling for most of the night instead of sleeping. My mind was flooded with so many questions. Why had Joe kept the old newspaper clipping about the beheading of Eduardo Cortez, head of Grande Distributors? Could he have been trying to escape the same men who had killed Cortez? Was that why he had changed his identity and moved to another country? Had the money in the Cayman Islands come from Cortez?

Although I didn't want to think about it, my mind also drifted to darker places. Could Joe have possibly committed a crime and then fled with someone else's money? It was hard to fathom such a possibility, but then everything I'd uncovered the past two days was unbelievable. I again wondered how my father-in-law could have even done such a thing as changing his identity. It's not like a man can stop in at his local government building and walk out a few minutes later as a new person. Joe had a birth certificate and a Social Security card. How was that possible? How was any of this possible? Around and around my mind went for hours.

So I was wide awake when my phone buzzed on my nightstand at eleven-thirty that night. With Taylor asleep next to me, I grabbed my phone, silenced the buzz, and squinted at the screen. It was not a number I recognized, but the area code told me it was Dallas. Slipping out of bed, I stepped out into the hallway and quietly answered it.

"Hello?"

"Alex? Alex Mahan?"

I recognized the familiar female voice. "Mrs. Tucker?"

"Yes, it's me. I'm so sorry to call you so late."

"No, it's fine. I'm up. What . . . what can I do for you?"

I moved farther down the hallway, away from the master bedroom, stepped inside my home office, and shut the door behind me.

"Well, you asked me to call you if I came across anything related to Joe, your father-in-law."

I perked up. "Did you?"

"Yes, I believe so. Earlier this evening, the police brought me Ethan's phone and some other personal items he had on him. I was looking on the phone a few minutes ago and came across a text exchange my husband had last night, just a few hours before he was killed. I think it has to do with your father-in-law."

"Can you screen capture it and text it to me?"

I quickly walked her through how to do that. A text photo arrived from her a moment later. The exchange was between Ethan and someone identified in his phone as Greta Malone. This really got my attention.

Ethan: Joe is dead.

Greta: I know. I'm in shock.

Ethan: Me, too. What are you going to do?

Greta: Lay low. Protect my husband.

Ethan: Does he know about Joe?

Greta: No. I need to keep it that way.

Ethan: Okay. Be safe.

Greta: You, too. I'll be in touch soon.

I had connected Greta and Ethan. I was not overly surprised. My gut told me the two of them had to be somehow intertwined with what happened with Joe. But I wondered what Greta had meant about protecting her husband. Was she talking about making sure he didn't discover an affair? That didn't make any sense to me. Why would Ethan know about it? Something else had to be in play here. I asked Sheila to give me the phone number listed for Greta Malone in Ethan's phone contacts. She did. It was the same DC number Greta had used to text Joe's phone earlier this week.

"What are they talking about, Alex?" Sheila asked me.

"I'm not sure. But I really appreciate you calling me."

"Of course."

We exchanged a couple of warm words and hung up.

Sitting at my desk, I opened my laptop and immediately typed *Greta Malone* into Google. It didn't take much searching for me to find a match. Greta Malone was married to a prominent DC business-man named Scott Malone who was currently running for Congress in Virginia. A photo of them together popped up on my screen. Although she was much older, of course, I felt certain she was the same attractive blonde woman I'd discovered in the old photos with my father-in-law. According to several news articles, Scott Malone was currently in a dead heat with the incumbent congressman with only three months left until election day. I went to Scott Malone's campaign website to see what else I could find. Scott's software analytics company had several high-profile corporate clients including American Express, GE, and even the CIA. I again thought about the photo of Greta standing on the CIA emblem. A profile page on the campaign website said Scott and Greta had been married fifteen years. Her husband had two adult children from a pre-vious marriage. There was no mention of Greta having any children of her own. There actually wasn't much written about Greta at all.

I began searching deeper, seeing if I could find out more about Greta—her history, previous employment, *something*. I searched through countless news articles, but everything was mainly focused on her husband and the election. I also couldn't find Greta Malone listed on *any* social media platforms or other common online forums.

I decided to call her phone number again. She had hung up on me before and then sent my next call to an automated voice mail. But maybe I'd get lucky this second time. I dialed her phone number and pressed "Call." Instead of getting Greta on the other end, I was immediately sent to an automated voice message saying the phone number was no longer in service. I squinted at my phone screen, double-checking the number, pressed "Call" again, and got the same automated message. Had she canceled her phone number after texting with Ethan just last night?

I tried to think of another way to contact her but couldn't find any other phone listings online. I again went to her husband's campaign website. Under a tab labeled *Events*, I found a campaign schedule. At noon tomorrow, Scott Malone would be doing a campaign stop inside a mall called Fashion Centre at Pentagon City near downtown DC. From what I could tell, Greta Malone had been accompanying her husband out on the campaign trail. Would she also be there tomorrow? Should I go find out? If I jumped on an early flight, I could easily make it.

I pondered that possibility and wondered how I would explain it to Taylor. I did have a somewhat plausible cover since one of our company's biggest clients was headquartered in DC. It would not be completely out of the realm of possibility for me to have to suddenly drop everything and fly up there tomorrow to keep them from leaving us for a competitor. I'd had to take a last-second flight to do something similar with another big client earlier this year.

Still, more lies, more deception. And I'd be again bolting on Taylor when I knew she really needed me. But how could I not pursue this if it meant finally getting to the truth about Joe? While it felt cruel to leave my wife alone right now, it felt foolish to stay put and do nothing. Sighing, I stood and walked to my office window, where I had a view of the street in front of our house. As I thought more about what I should do, my eyes drifted across our well-landscaped front lawn and then settled on a vehicle I spotted parked on the curb a half block up the street. I leaned in closer to the window, then cursed. A black Ford Explorer. My heart started racing. Squinting, I thought I could make out wisps of smoke coming from a crack in the driver's-side window. Someone was sitting in the vehicle right now, smoking a cigarette and watching my house. I thought about the man who had killed Ethan and then about my girls sleeping upstairs. I suddenly felt a fierce surge of both fear and protectiveness.

I moved quickly, bolting out of my office, and headed straight into the garage. I found one of my baseball bats mixed in with other sports equipment. Then I opened the garage door and walked briskly down the driveway and into the street. No way in hell was I going to let someone sit out here on my street, watching my house while my family slept only fifty feet away. I was not hiding the fact that I was coming straight for whoever was in the vehicle. But I still couldn't get a good look at who was behind the wheel. As if sensing what was happening, the driver started the vehicle and flipped on bright headlights. I was blinded for a moment. Then the driver punched the gas and did a swift U-turn in the street. I jumped back out of the way so I wouldn't get clipped. The engine roared, and the vehicle's tires spun. Seconds later, the car was gone around another street corner.

Was it the same guy who had shot and killed Ethan Tucker?

Could it have been the man with the navy tattoo?

I wasn't sure. But I could feel my heart pounding in my chest.

TWENTY-FIVE

I woke Taylor early to deliver the unexpected travel news. I explained how I'd received an alarming late-night email from one of our biggest clients and felt I had no choice but to go see them in person today in order to salvage the relationship. At first, she let me have it. *How could I take off today? She was already so overwhelmed. This was the worst possible timing!* But then she gradually calmed down, telling me, "I guess our lives and work have to go on, in spite of everything that's happened this week." I promised her it would just be a day trip. I'd be back home and in bed with her by the end of the night. Plus, I suggested the long flight would give me the additional time I needed to finish the photo presentation. At least that part was true. Then I kissed her, went upstairs and kissed the girls, who were still asleep, and headed for the airport.

Once in the air, I resisted the urge to go back to sleep myself since I'd barely gotten a wink after the incident outside my house. I kept getting up last night and checking the front windows. Thankfully, I never spotted the black Explorer again.

Pulling out my laptop, I began working on the presentation. For the next couple of hours, I pored through thousands of digital family photos, looking for those special gems of my father-in-law. It was a surreal exercise with everything going through my mind right now. The photos on my laptop screen told a story of a faithful and committed family man who had been there for every moment of my life over the past sixteen years. Joe had been present at every single one of my girls' birthday parties, school plays, sporting events, and dance recitals. Every backyard barbecue and swim party. Every Halloween, Thanksgiving, and Christmas. Nearly every vacation. My girls had not celebrated a single event in their lives without Papa being there with a front-row seat. Neither had I. The weight of reality hit me again, and tears began to well in my eyes. I did not know at the moment how to balance the shock of my recent discovery with the pain that still filled my heart about his loss.

I shut my laptop and stared out the plane window as the sun slowly rose into the eastern sky. Sitting there, I began to realize how much I'd used this pursuit of truth behind our family money the past two days as a desperate distraction from having to deal with my own personal heartache. I didn't want to think about how much I already missed Joe. I didn't want to admit how scared I felt about having to lead my family forward without him in the seat next to me. I had relied on him for so much. Joe had been like a lighthouse for me, always bringing me safely back to shore. None of this new discovery made any sense to me. Why would Joe have done this? He must have had a legitimate reason. He must have gotten caught up in something with his murdered Mexican client that compelled him to go on the run. But I couldn't reconcile the plane crash that killed Joe's father and the millions of dollars he had hidden in the Caymans that he'd used to fund my company. Was that money stolen? How much more was still out there? Is that what eventually caught up with Joe and Ethan and got them both killed?

My thoughts were interrupted by my phone buzzing in my pocket. I had used the in-flight Wi-Fi option to stay connected with my messages. I pulled it out and found a new text message from Raul in Matamoros.

Raul: I've made an ID on the man in the photo. His name is Antonio Perez. He's a CNI agent.

I pitched my head. CNI agent? I quickly searched on my phone and discovered the CNI, or the Centro Nacional de Inteligencia, was Mexico's equivalent of the CIA. This caused me to curse out loud, which caught the attention of the sixtysomething woman who was trying to sleep in the seat next to me. She peered over, gave me a seriously wrinkled frown. I apologized before going back to my phone.

I quickly responded to Raul.

Me: CNI? What is going on?

Raul: I don't know yet. And I'm getting serious pushback from my superiors about why I'm even asking questions about this guy. Something is clearly up. I'll keep you posted.

Me: Gracias.

I eased back into my seat, fought the urge to curse again. Why would someone from Mexican intelligence be involved in Joe's and Ethan's deaths?

TWENTY-SIX

My plane touched down midmorning at Reagan National. Once inside the airport, I made a quick phone call to the *El Paso Times* because it looked as if the same reporter who had written the story about the murder of Joe's old client thirty-five years ago was now one of the newspaper's senior editors. I asked a receptionist to speak to Felix Rodriguez and was thankfully put right through to him.

"This is Felix," answered a hoarse voice on the other end.

"Felix, my name's Alex Mahan. This may be a long shot, but are you the same Felix Rodriguez who wrote a story in the *El Paso Times* thirty-five years ago about the beheading of a businessman named Eduardo Cortez?"

He kind of laughed. "Well, that's a blast from the past. But, yes, I wrote that. Why're you asking?"

"Digging up information for a lawyer here. Cortez was an old client. Just need a minute of your time to ask a couple of questions."

"A minute is all I've got, pal. So fire away."

"You remember much about the happenings around that murder?"

"Not much. But I remember it was one of the worst crime scenes I'd ever covered."

"Was anyone ever prosecuted?"

"Nope. But it seemed pretty clear it was the work of one of the cartels."

"Why? Was Cortez known to be involved with the cartels?"

"Not necessarily. But most men who ran successful businesses around here at that time were tied to the cartels in one form or another. Plus, you know, they cut off his damn head. Only the cartels would do something like that. Usually as a warning to others."

"Any idea why they killed him?"

"Nothing was ever verified. But there was a rumor back then that either he or someone working with him had stolen fifty million dollars."

"Wow. Fifty million?"

"Yeah, that'll get your head chopped off around here real quick."

"I bet."

"Look, I gotta get on another call. We done?"

"One more question. You remember anything about a plane crash around that same time that killed two lawyers from Dallas?"

"Nope."

"Okay, thanks for your time."

Hanging up, I felt a chill race down my spine. Had Joe somehow gotten his hands on $50 million and then disappeared? Had he held on to it all these years? Was it stolen cartel money that had funded my company and created a brand-new life for Taylor and me? Were they still searching for that money? I desperately needed to talk to Greta today. She was the only hope I still had for putting the pieces of this dark and crazy puzzle together.

After renting a small car, I drove straight to the historic Hay-Adams hotel, just a block north of the White House, where I knew from reviewing his credit card statement that Joe had stayed on his recent trip to DC. I wanted to see if I could find out any details about what he did while in town or, more important, whom he was with while at the hotel. I parked along a curb, made my way inside the hotel lobby, and sidled up to a front-desk clerk a moment later.

"Checking in?" the young man asked me.

"No, I'm actually looking for some information about my father-in-law, who stayed here about ten days ago."

"What kind of information, sir?"

"I was hoping someone on the hotel staff might be able to give me some insight on whether they saw him here with anyone. Can I show you a photo?"

"Well, I'm not really supposed to talk about hotel guests. It goes against our privacy policy."

"Look, I understand that. And I know this is an odd request. But my father-in-law was killed a few days ago. My family is in tremendous shock and looking for answers. I'm the executor of his estate. I can show you paperwork, if you want. I just need some help."

"Oh my gosh, I'm so sorry." He took a glance over his shoulder, like he might be checking to see if his manager was around. "What was his name?"

"Joe Dobson." I showed him a photo on my phone. "Do you recognize him?"

He studied my phone, shook his head. "No, I don't think so. But other than checking guests in and out, I don't really have too much involvement with them. Plus, I only work four shifts a week." He typed on his computer, squinted at the screen. "Yeah, I wasn't even working when your father-in-law was staying here with us. Sorry."

I took a shot in the dark. "Can you tell me if someone named Greta Malone was a guest here at that same time?"

"Like I said, I'm not allowed—"

"Come on, help me out. It'll take you two seconds to check, and then I'll leave you alone."

The clerk gave another quick glance over his shoulder, then typed on his keyboard. "No Greta Malone."

"Anyone else around here you think might be helpful to me?"

"The most connected person here is Ms. Marley. She runs a bar downstairs called Off The Record. The bar is closed right now, but she usually comes in early to get things rolling."

"Thanks. I appreciate that."

I found my way down to an upscale lounge that basically felt hidden in the basement of the hotel. As the clerk suggested, the bar was currently closed, but I did see some activity in the back. I navigated the oversize wingback chairs sitting below brass chandeliers and noticed all the caricatures of political figures on the walls. A young guy with a well-trimmed beard wearing a white button-down shirt and a gray vest was stacking up glasses behind the bar.

"How're you doing?" I said, stepping up to the bar.

"Good, man. We don't open for a bit."

"I know. Any chance Ms. Marley is around?"

He nodded over his shoulder. "In the back."

"You mind asking her if I can have a moment?"

"She's a little busy right now."

He didn't seem overly eager to be helpful. I reached into my pocket, took out some cash, and placed a twenty-dollar bill on the bar. "I'd really appreciate it."

He eyeballed it for only a second before snagging it. "You got a name?"

"Alex. But she doesn't know me."

After stuffing the twenty in his pocket, he walked to a door into the back of the bar and disappeared. I stood there for a few minutes, wondering if the guy had taken my money and just gone for a smoke break. But finally, a woman in probably her late forties with bleached blonde hair, wearing the same white shirt and gray vest combo, appeared from the back.

"You looking for me?" she asked.

She had a raspy smoker's voice.

"You're Ms. Marley?"

"Depends. What do you want?"

"I come in peace, I promise. I'm just looking for some answers about my father-in-law, who was killed earlier this week. He stayed here at the hotel about ten days ago. I wondered if he might have come into the bar."

My explanation seemed to disarm some of her initial skepticism about me. Ms. Marley made her way closer to me and stood behind the bar. "How was he killed, if you don't mind my asking?"

"We were on a family trip to Mexico. He was kidnapped. We found him dead the next day."

"Sorry to hear that. But what does that have to do with my bar?"

"I'm not sure. I think his death might somehow be connected to some people he met with while he was in DC."

"You have a photo?"

I nodded, pulled up a photo of Joe on my phone, showed it to her. Ms. Marley tilted her head, her shoulder sagging. "No, really?"

"You recognize him?"

"Yeah, I do. He gave me a monster tip."

"Joe was a very generous man."

"Yeah, he was a sweet guy. He got me talking about my daughter, and I told him how I was struggling to pay for her college tuition. I think his bill was only, like, thirty dollars or something. But his tip was for five hundred. He wrote a nice little note, wishing me and my daughter the best of luck. Sucks to hear a guy like that is no longer with us."

"Was he in here by himself?"

She shook her head. "No."

I pulled up another photo on my phone of Greta Malone, taken from a recent campaign event. "Was he with her?"

Ms. Marley stared at the photo. "Yep. They sat over there at that table." She pointed toward a booth against the wall. "There were two other guys with them."

This caught my attention. "Really?"

"Yeah. It looked like serious business. They weren't laughing it up and telling stories like most others do in here."

I wondered if one of the guys could've been Ethan Tucker. I had not thought to ask Sheila Tucker if Ethan had taken a recent trip to DC. On my phone, I quickly went back to the website for Ethan's financial firm, pulled up his profile page, which had thankfully not yet been taken down, and showed it to Ms. Marley. "Was this one of the guys?"

"Yep."

"What did the other guy look like?"

"Bald with a thick mustache. Decent shape. About your height. Maybe a few years younger than your father-in-law. He was the first one here and sat at the end of the bar for a bit until the others arrived."

Bald with a thick mustache? I thought of the guy who had followed me around downtown and whom I'd spotted with me in Dallas yesterday.

"Probably a long shot, but any chance you noticed if the bald guy had a crossed-cannons navy tattoo on his left wrist?"

"Bingo. That's the guy. I notice everything, hon. I even asked him about it because my brother served in the navy."

"You get his name?"

She shrugged. "Maybe. But I don't recall it."

"Damn," I muttered. My mind started trying to connect the dots. Who was this guy? He was clearly following me around for some reason. Why? If he was both in Austin and then in Dallas with me, could he also now be in DC?

"Finding this guy important to you?" Ms. Marley asked.

"Yeah, I think so."

"Give me a second."

Ms. Marley disappeared behind the door to the back. While waiting, I thought about calling Sheila Tucker to find out if she knew why Ethan was in DC ten days ago. But I didn't want to upset the woman beyond the grief she was already experiencing. A text arrived on my phone from Taylor, checking in with me and wanting to know how things were going with my client. I sent her a quick response, telling her I was just about to go in to meet with them. She "hearted" my reply and sent a follow-up text saying they'd be crazy to leave someone like me. I "hearted" her message in return. Then my shoulders dropped. How long could I keep up this lying?

I again thought about the meeting Joe had here with the three others. Had all four of them been involved with whatever happened with Joe's client thirty-five years ago and the stolen money that had pushed my father-in-law to go completely off the grid?

Ms. Marley reappeared from the back, walked over to the bar, and handed me a scrap of paper with something written on it. She'd scribbled down a name: *Al Del Luca.*

I looked up at her. "Tattoo guy?"

She nodded. "He paid his bar tab with a credit card."

"I really appreciate this."

"No sweat. I feel like I owe your father-in-law something. The man helped keep my baby girl in school this next semester."

I returned to the hotel lobby, grabbed a chair in a quiet corner, and began searching Google for the name *Al Del Luca* on my phone. It was a unique enough name to not have to wade through several pages of hits. But I still couldn't find much. Nothing on social media or LinkedIn. But I did find a mention of an Al and Gloria Del Luca on a DC city data website that listed a property valuation on a small single-family home in the metro area. Jumping onto Facebook, I searched for *Gloria Del Luca* instead. A page of a woman with black hair who lived in DC and looked to be about the same age as the man with the tattoo appeared. About halfway down her page, I spotted a photo of Gloria with the same man who'd been following me around the past couple of days. I quickly went back over to the property valuation web page. The property appraisal on the single-family home was from over five years ago. I wondered if the Del Lucas still lived at the residence. I clicked on a link, and it brought up a pin location on a map. The house was about twenty minutes from the hotel. There was only one way to find out.

TWENTY-SEVEN

The pin in the map led me to a neighborhood called Woodridge, where I parked in front of an old gray-brick house with a small front porch, a nothing yard, and no garage—just a short driveway leading up to a simple carport. I sat in my rental car for a few minutes and studied the house. There were no vehicles in the driveway or under the carport. Did that mean no one was home? I had hoped to find Gloria Del Luca here and perhaps talk my way into getting more information about her husband. I checked my rearview mirror. There were no cars behind me on the street. On the entire drive out of DC proper, I'd been monitoring my mirrors, wondering if Del Luca could have possibly followed me from Austin back to DC and was now watching me stare at his own house. But I saw no signs of anyone staying on my tail. I'd even circled the streets of this neighborhood a couple of times to be sure.

I got out of the rental car, moved toward the house, and trotted up the porch steps to the front door. Before knocking, I took a casual peek in the front window. I didn't see any signs of movement inside. I gave three firm raps on the door, waited. I heard nothing. I rang the doorbell. Still nothing. A black mailbox hung on the brick next to the front door, so I reached inside and found a few mail items. A utility bill, a women's magazine, and some junk mail. All were addressed to either Gloria or Al Del Luca. This at least confirmed they still lived here. I wondered what to do next. I needed to know more about Del Luca and how he was involved in my father-in-law's situation. I couldn't just turn around and leave. There had to be answers inside. But what was I supposed to do? Break into the house? I glanced behind me, looking for nosy neighbors. Then I put my hand on the door handle and tried to turn it. Locked. I was almost relieved. Was I really willing to walk right into a stranger's house?

Turning around, I eased down the front steps but paused on the sidewalk before returning to my rental car. Would the back door also be locked? I briskly walked up the driveway toward the carport, where I found a wooden gate to the backyard of the house. No lock on it. I clicked the latch on the gate, pushed it slightly open, glanced inside. Thankfully, no signs of any dogs. As I stepped through the gate, my heart started racing a bit. Because the house had neighbors on both sides, I felt exposed with each step up a gravel path to a back door. Cupping my hands together, I peered inside a small window in the middle of the door. A laundry room that led into the kitchen. I put my hand on the door handle and tried to turn it. Also locked. I cursed. But then my eyes drifted down to several potted plants situated right outside the back door.

Kneeling, I began shifting pots around to see if any of them might have a spare key hidden beneath them. I found a key under the fourth pot. Now my heart was really pumping. It was one thing to step inside someone's backyard. That didn't quite feel like a crime. But it was another thing to use their key to enter their house uninvited. Everything sensible in me told me to turn around and leave. But I was desperate for answers. Joe was killed for a reason. I had to know that reason. So I put the spare key in the lock and turned the door handle. The door opened. Before I could talk myself out of it, I slipped inside and shut the door behind me.

I quickly went to work. If I was going to commit this crime, I was going to at least get in and out as fast as possible. I hustled through the laundry room and into the kitchen, looking for anything that might tell me more about Al Del Luca. There was a stack of opened mail on the counter. I rummaged through it but found only common bills and such. I ducked into the next room, found a dining table with a half-finished puzzle of the Eiffel Tower. Another hallway led me to the living room, where I felt the most uncomfortable because of the front window. I paused to look outside and make sure no one was coming up to the house. There wasn't much of anything downstairs, so I found the stairs and bound up two steps at a time. There were three bedrooms upstairs. I entered what looked like the master with a king-size bed and two nightstands. On one nightstand was a stack of romance novels. I circled the bed and searched the other nightstand. There were a couple of Tom Clancy novels and several sports magazines. But still nothing that told me much about Del Luca, other than he liked sports and thrillers.

Stepping through the master bathroom, I entered a long and cluttered closet. It was stuffed full of hanging clothes. On one side hung an assortment of dresses and colorful sweaters. On the other side were slacks, jeans, button-downs, sport coats. I sorted through the men's clothes, searched a few pockets on the sport coats, but didn't find anything of relevance. At the end of the closet was a tall dresser. Sitting on top of the dresser was a jewelry box filled with women's costume jewelry. There was also a clay bowl with cuff links, some random keys, loose change, and *finally* something that mattered to me—an ID card stuck inside a plastic holder with a metal clip on it. Picking up the ID card, I stared at a profile photo of Al Del Luca. Then I read where he worked: *Central Intelligence Agency, United States of America.*

CIA? The guy was CIA? The rest of the ID card showed several clearance codes and other assorted security information. I took out my phone, snapped a quick photo of the front of the ID card. Why were Joe, Greta, and Ethan meeting with a CIA agent? And why was the same agent now following me? I again thought about the old photo in Joe's small safe box that showed Greta standing on the CIA emblem. But there had been zero mention of her being CIA in anything related to her husband's campaign. What the hell was going on? Could Joe have secretly been CIA? It would certainly add credence to how he managed to go from being Daniel Gibson to Joe Dobson. But it still didn't feel right. I'd never noticed any odd behavior from my father-in-law that told me he could have had a secret career as an intelligence officer. Joe didn't even travel much.

I suddenly heard a door open and shut somewhere downstairs. Panic gripped me. Someone else was inside the house. And I was standing in a closet upstairs about as far removed from an exit as possible. What should I do? I stepped back into the master bedroom, listened. I thought I could hear activity downstairs in the kitchen. Was it Gloria Del Luca? Or was it the CIA agent himself? Would he be carrying a gun? Was I about to get myself shot? I rushed over to the bedroom window, peered into the backyard. Right below the window was a concrete patio with a table and several lawn chairs. I considered it for a moment. The drop wouldn't kill me, but I might break an ankle or something. I wasn't ready to do that just yet. There had to be an easier way out of the house.

Moving out into the hallway, I stood a few feet away from the top of the stairs. I could hear things more clearly now. The noise was definitely coming from the kitchen. Sounded like grocery bags being unpacked. The kitchen did not have a direct view to the front door. I wondered if I could quietly manage my way down the stairs and leave straight out the front without being caught. It was risky. But how else was I going to get out of here? I couldn't hide in a closet all day. One careful step at a time, I began to descend the stairs. The old wood creaked beneath my feet. I had to pause with each step and wait to see if the noise drew suspicion from the kitchen. I eventually made it all the way to the bottom. My heart was pounding, and sweat was dripping from my forehead.

I took a step toward the front door and then froze in place when I heard whoever was in the kitchen enter the dining room. I had a split second to make my next move. I knew there was a clear view of the front door from the dining room. That was no longer an option. And I sure as hell wasn't going all the way back upstairs. So I stepped fully into the short hallway of the downstairs and pressed my back against the wall. On one end of the hallway was the front door and living room. On the other end was the kitchen. Directly behind me, on the opposite side of the wall, was the dining room. I could hear whoever was in the house messing around in that room. I felt stuck in limbo until the person made a move in one direction or the other. A phone rang loudly in the dining room and sent a shiver straight up my spine. Then I heard a female voice answer. It had to be the wife, Gloria.

"Hey, honey."

A pause.

"What do you mean someone is in the house?"

I stiffened. Who knew I was here? Del Luca? But how? I searched the walls and ceiling corners for security cameras but didn't spot anything. There were no alarm beeps when I'd entered. How would anyone know I was inside? But if this guy was CIA, I supposed he could have other resources providing security. I felt the panic inside me start to run wild. I had to get out right now.

"You got an alert on your phone?" I heard Gloria say. "I don't hear anything in the house." A pause. "Yes, I'll go look around."

Staying perfectly still, I listened closely to see which direction Gloria chose to go first. I heard her say "I *am* hurrying" from the living room. I moved to my left, opposite from Gloria, stepped farther down the hallway, and slipped inside the kitchen just as she entered the same hallway where I'd been hiding. Wasting little time in the kitchen, I quickly moved to the back door, cautiously opened it, and then darted outside. I was through the backyard gate and out onto the driveway a couple of seconds later. I noticed a white Honda Pilot now parked under the carport. Tucked in beside the neighbor's fence, I carefully moved up the driveway toward the street. I didn't take another breath until I was inside my rental car again and racing out of the neighborhood.

TWENTY-EIGHT

Thirty minutes later, I stood in the center courtyard of a glitzy four-story mall called Fashion Centre at Pentagon City, where Greta's husband, Scott Malone, was scheduled to have a campaign event in a few minutes. There was a small stage set up in the middle of the courtyard with about ten rows of chairs. Campaign signs were posted everywhere, and already a crowd of about a hundred or so people had gathered. So far, I'd seen no trace of Scott or Greta Malone. They were probably off getting last-minute makeup and such done before stepping up on the small stage and pandering for votes. I was very eager to finally put real eyes on the mystery woman who had first entered into this equation by sending the text to Joe's phone before I even knew he was dead.

I again thought about that text. *Call me ASAP. I think we've been found out.* Who was she talking about? *Who* had found them out? Mexican intelligence? A drug cartel? The CIA? Two of the people who had been in the bar at the Hay-Adams hotel the other day were now dead. Was Greta Malone in danger, too? I had no way of knowing without speaking with the woman. I sure as hell hoped she would be here today.

My phone buzzed in my pocket. I looked at the number calling me and recognized it as an El Paso area code. This got my attention. I had left a voice mail for a man named Blake Crosby a few hours ago. According to the *Dallas Times Herald* news article I'd found in the SMU archives, a man by that same name had been a technician at the small airfield the day the plane carrying Bruce and Daniel Gibson had crashed thirty-five years ago. I'd searched for the name in El Paso and happened to find someone who presented himself as a handyman and mechanic who—based off a picture in a cheap ad—looked like he was old enough to have been at the airfield on that day.

"This is Alex," I said, answering the phone.

"Hey, did you call looking for a handyman?"

I hadn't explained myself on the phone. "Is this Blake Crosby?"

"Yes, sir, at your service. What can I do for you?"

"I have a strange question for you, Mr. Crosby. Any chance you used to work at Burnett Airfield thirty-five years ago?"

"That is a strange question. But the answer is yes. How the heck did you know that?"

"I read an old newspaper story about a plane crash that killed two lawyers back when you used to work there. You were quoted in the story."

"I'll be damned. I do remember talking to a couple of reporters. But I never got a chance to read anything about it."

"Do you remember much about the day that plane crashed?"

"Well, sure. Not every day you see a plane explode right in front of your eyes. It would've been pretty spectacular had it not been so damn tragic."

"Where were you when you saw it happen?"

"You a reporter or something?"

"No, but I think I have a family connection to the two men who were killed."

"Oh, I see. Well, I was over in a small hangar working on a prop plane. Looked up and watched a Cessna 152 that was just on the runway glide up into the air. Everything looked fine. Then all of a sudden, it just exploded. I mean, it was a real fireball. All of this debris just went everywhere."

"Did you happen to see the two men before they climbed into the plane?"

"I did. They walked through the hangar over to where the plane was parked."

This made me perk up. "Could you describe them to me?"

"Well, hell, now you're really testing my memory. But I think one guy was probably fiftysomething. He wore a business suit and carried a briefcase, which I found kind of funny as he climbed into a little two-seater. I only found out later he was a lawyer."

"What about the other guy?"

"He was a lot younger. Probably in his twenties."

"Was he also in a business suit?"

"Nope. Just plain street clothes. Jeans and a T-shirt."

That seemed odd. Why would Joe have been dressed down? "Did the younger guy kind of look like the older guy? They were father and son."

"Hard to say. The older guy was clean-shaven. The younger guy had a thick beard."

A beard? There were no photos of my father-in-law at that age with a beard. So who the hell got in the plane with Joe's dad? Where was Joe?

"Mr. Crosby, are you sure both men got on the plane that day?"

"Yep. Watched them both climb inside and set off down the runway."

"You're an expert mechanic, wouldn't you say?" I asked Crosby.

"Well, I don't know about that. But I've certainly seen a lot of engines in my sixty-five years."

"I bet. The newspaper implied that the plane exploded because of mechanical failure. Is that what you also saw that day?"

"Funny you should ask me that. Because to me, it looked more like a bomb exploded than an engine failing. But what the hell do I know?"

TWENTY-NINE

The campaign event started about fifteen minutes late. The crowd had grown bigger. I estimated around two hundred people, although it was hard to tell who actually showed up for the event and who were just curious mall shoppers. I figured that was part of the reason to hold a campaign stop here. A candidate could draw a lot of extra eyeballs. I stood in the back of the crowd, waiting for Scott and Greta Malone to step out onstage. Someone in a suit finally walked up to a microphone and gave an over-the-top welcome to who he called the next congressman from the Eighth Congressional District of Virginia. Then I spotted the couple appear from off to the right and step up onto the stage.

I felt a wave of relief pour through me that Greta was here today with her husband. Because I had to be back in Austin tonight for Joe's service tomorrow, I did not have the luxury of bouncing to every campaign event over the next few days, waiting for Greta to show up. The woman looked much younger than her nearly sixty years of age. Her hair was blonde and pinned back. She wore a blue dress with a USA pin on the front. Her husband had short black and gray-speckled hair and wore a dark blue suit with a red tie. The crowd cheered while patriotic music played on some speakers. I looked up and noticed more people stopping on the floors above us and staring down into the courtyard.

Scott and Greta waved for a bit, then kissed, and Greta walked off the stage to the right again. She huddled with a short woman with silver hair in a black pantsuit. I began to move around the crowd in Greta's direction.

From the podium, Malone began to give the kind of speech I'd heard countless times from others running for office. Positive change and reform on this and that issue with what felt like planted clapping throughout. I continued to weave closer to Greta's side of the crowd. She was about fifty feet away from me. I noticed a man in a black suit right behind her who looked like he could break a telephone pole in two. I figured he might be some kind of security. Not only was Scott Malone running for office, he was also very wealthy. I studied Greta without being too conspicuous, wondering what role she played in all this mystery surrounding Joe. She had clearly been there in the beginning, when my father in law went from being Daniel Gibson to Joe Dobson. And now I knew she was also there at the end of his life. What had happened in between? Had they stayed connected all these years? What brought them together in DC ten days ago?

Scott went on and on in his speech. I had to admit, he had a dynamic presence onstage and made for a good political candidate. I figured at this point I would need to wait until the speech was over and everything was concluded to get my opportunity to approach Greta. I wondered what kind of reaction she would have when she found out I was Joe's son-in-law. She had hung up on me the first time we'd spoken. Would she be more open to a discussion this time around? I had no idea what to expect but would find out soon.

I tuned out Scott's campaign promises and again thought about what Blake Crosby, the mechanic from El Paso, had just told me on the phone about the plane crash thirty-five years ago. *It looked more like a bomb exploded than an engine falling apart.* I wondered if that was possible. Could someone have put a bomb on the plane? But how did Joe escape it? Did he know not to get on the plane?

It seemed like Scott was beginning to wrap up his talk. My eyes shifted from the stage over to Greta again. I stiffened. She was staring right at me. Or she at least appeared to be. Did she somehow recognize me? I kind of raised my hand, a very casual wave, but she quickly looked away. Maybe she wasn't looking at me. But it sure as hell seemed like it. My eyes went back to the stage, as Scott concluded his speech with "God bless Virginia. And God bless the USA." The crowd erupted, and the music began blaring again.

When I looked back over toward Greta, she was no longer standing there. I took a few steps to my right, peering around a crowd that was suddenly moving, trying to put eyes on her. That's when I spotted her. She was not staying at the campaign event. She was hurriedly retreating down the mall corridor all by herself.

I stepped forward, began weaving through the fifty or so people who separated me from the other side of the event. I had to get to Greta before I lost sight of her. Moving more quickly, I ducked in and around several people until I found a clearing into the rest of the mall. The crowd behind me was still cheering. I noticed that Scott had not yet left the stage. Why would Greta stay for the whole speech and then bolt right before it ended? Had I spooked her? She was up ahead of me about a hundred feet, swiftly walking down a corridor lined with retail stores. I would need to move even faster to catch up with her. I thought about yelling out her name but decided that would be a bit awkward. Instead, I began to do a light jog.

When I was within forty feet, I called out, "Greta!"

She turned, gave a quick glance behind her. I put my hand up, letting her know it came from me, but she didn't acknowledge it. Spinning back around, she turned right at the next mall corridor and disappeared from my view for a moment. I kept hustling forward and turned down the same corridor a few seconds later. Then I paused. I couldn't spot her anywhere. Where did she go? To my direct right was a women's clothing store. I hurried up to the entrance, peered inside, but didn't see her among the shoppers and racks of clothes. I moved to the next store—a high-end women's shoe shop. Again, I searched everywhere but couldn't find Greta. I twisted back around and stared across the corridor to the stores on the opposite side. But there was no sign of her. I'd only lost sight of her for a couple of seconds. Where the hell did she go?

For the next five minutes, I kept going store to store up the corridor but didn't find her inside any of them. Frustrated, I decided to return to the campaign event. Although I doubted it, I wondered if I'd missed that she'd circled back and returned to her husband. When I got back to the courtyard, the crowd had mostly dispersed. There was no sign of Scott or Greta Malone anywhere. But I did see the woman with silver hair in the black pantsuit. She was walking away in the opposite direction from the stage.

I hurried up to her. "Excuse me, are you with the campaign?"

She turned. "Yes."

"I'm trying to get in touch with Greta Malone. Do you think you can help me out? I really need to speak with her today."

"And you are?"

I wondered how to answer that. "A friend of a friend."

She kind of pitched her head slightly, as if she'd already dismissed me as someone irrelevant. "We appreciate your support, sir. But Ms. Malone is a very busy woman."

"Look, I'm not some kind of stalker or anything. But I have to talk to her."

The woman kind of rolled her eyes. "Why don't you give me your name and number? I'll be sure to pass the message along."

I knew that was a lie. She was just getting rid of me. Just the same, I told her my name and phone number, and she at least pretended to type it into her phone. Then we parted ways. Sighing, I stood there wondering what the hell had just happened. I'd been only a few steps behind Greta. I'd only lost sight of her for maybe three seconds. I was certain she saw me. We had connected eyes. Greta knew it was me who had called out her name. So why did she flee? And how could she have just vanished like that?

THIRTY

My plane ride back to Austin was a serious mental and emotional balancing act. On one hand, I was trying to process what all I'd discovered while in DC and what had just taken place with Greta Malone's disappearing act; on the other hand, I had to somehow focus enough to finish the video presentation for Joe's service tomorrow. No matter how crazy everything felt right now, I had to be faithful to Taylor, Carol, and both of my girls, and make sure I presented Joe in the best way possible.

The girls were already asleep when I finally got home. Taylor was in our bedroom, packing for our trip out to the lake house after her father's service tomorrow. The bed was covered in stacks of clothes to be placed into suitcases. I kissed Taylor on the cheek, then dropped into a leather reading chair we had situated in the corner of our bedroom, feeling exhausted.

"How were the girls tonight?" I asked her.

"Mostly happy. They're very excited to go out to the lake. But I don't think they really know what to make of the service tomorrow. We've never taken them to a funeral. So for their first to be their own grandfather is going to be heavy, I think."

"They are surprisingly resilient."

"I know. Maybe I'm more concerned about me." She placed a stack of clothes into one of two suitcases. "So did you save the day? Is your client staying?"

"Too soon to know."

"What does that mean?"

"It means I'll be delayed in going out to the lake house for a day or two."

She looked over, huffed. "Are you serious?"

"I'll try to wrap it up as quickly as possible, Taylor."

There was no way I could go out to the lake right now. I had to keep pressing forward in my pursuit of the truth. Although I wasn't sure yet of my next move, I knew I couldn't do anything stuck at the lake with my family. I could tell Taylor was more than just annoyed. She was understandably pissed. I had rarely put work above family over the past three years. To do it now when she was at her most vulnerable was probably very confusing. I had prepared what I felt was a viable counterattack in anticipation of this exact response from her. I hoped it would soften the blow.

"This sucks, Alex. You've basically been MIA for the past two days. And now you're going to skip out on us again?"

"I don't really have a choice, babe."

"Sure you do. Tell your client to screw off."

"You don't really mean that."

She let out a deep sigh, her shoulders sagging. "I know. It's just . . ." Another heavy sigh. "I'm just ready for this to all be over already. I don't even know how I'm going to get through tomorrow."

"I know what will probably make it easier."

"What?"

"If you watch the video with me tonight instead of tomorrow."

"You finished it?"

"Yes. Wasn't easy. Lots of big emotions. But I think you'll like it. How about we take a break from packing and go watch it together?"

"Okay."

A few minutes later, Taylor and I sat together on our oversize sofa in the media room. Taylor snuggled in really close to me, as if she were about to watch a scary move and didn't want to look directly at the screen. I could feel the apprehension she was carrying in her whole body. After dimming the lights, I pressed "Play," the music started, and the first photo of her dad appeared on the screen. It was taken two years ago at Easter. He was kneeling behind Olivia and Nicole, his arms wrapped around each of them. Our girls had the biggest smiles on their faces. So did Joe. He looked so happy. It's how I wanted to remember him. I wondered if there was any pathway forward that would allow that to happen for me. I couldn't see it at the moment. More photos filled the screen. Within seconds, Taylor was sobbing. And so was I.

THIRTY-ONE

I got a call from Raul the next morning while Taylor and I were out handling some last-minute details before Joe's funeral service. We were inside Nordstrom department store, looking for hair bows for our girls. I was committed to being with my wife every minute of today all the way through the funeral service. She deserved at least that from me after the last couple of days. I told Taylor the call was from my client in DC and then drifted off into a quiet corner to answer it.

After a quick greeting, Raul got straight to it. "I brought in one of the guys involved in Joe's abduction. I actually didn't know he was involved—we brought him in on another charge—but then he hinted to me that he had information about my other case. He wanted to cut a deal. Of course, we don't cut deals down here, so we just squeezed him a bit until he popped right open."

"What did he say?"

"Said a guy paid him and a couple of his buddies a hundred thousand pesos to grab your father-in-law, put him in the van, and bring him to a certain location. I showed him a photo of Antonio Perez. He confirmed that was the guy who paid him."

"Did he know anything about the explosion?"

"No, he said they bound Joe in the back of the van, drove to a certain parking lot, and then left the vehicle with Joe inside, as instructed. He doesn't know what happened to him after they all walked away."

"You believe him?"

"*Sí*. Like I said, amigo, we squeezed him. Believe me, he had no secrets left when we were done with him."

I figured *squeezed him* meant a good beating. Out of necessity, I imagined they might do law enforcement a little different south of the border.

"If this was truly a CNI effort, Raul, why would Perez hire out local thugs?"

"They do it all the time. Deniability. If things go wrong, there's nothing that leads back to them. The guy we brought in had no idea who he was or that he was an agent of the CNI. To him, he was just a rich guy."

With both the CNI and the CIA somehow involved in this deal, I again wondered if Joe had been part of some kind of international intelligence operation that had put him in a crisis situation. Could the $50 million have actually been stolen from the Mexican government instead of a drug cartel?

"Have you been able to pick up any other noise about CNI involvement?" I asked Raul. "Outside of Antonio Perez?"

"No, not yet. I have a couple of connections with the CNI. But neither of them was able to give me any insider info about this. They know nothing. One of my contacts—my sister's brother-in-law—was going to look deeper into it for me. But I do have some other trouble on my end."

"What's that?"

"My boss just ordered me to drop this whole thing. He actually threatened to fire me if I didn't let this thing go and get back to work on other cases."

"Damn, Raul, I'm sorry. What are you going to do?"

"Disobey that order and press forward. I made a vow to God and my city to uphold my duties as an officer of the law. I'll just have to be very careful, amigo."

"I'm glad to hear you say that. I'd be lost on this thing without you. Do you think there's any chance Perez could be acting independently from the CNI?"

"I thought about that, too. But I can't find any real reason for it. Perez doesn't need the money. His uncle is a super-wealthy businessman down in Mexico City."

This caught my attention. "Who's his uncle?"

"Miguel Cortez. He's head of a company called Grande Distributors."

THIRTY-TWO

I felt so distracted as I got dressed in a black suit in our master bathroom and prepared to head over to Joe's funeral service at the church. I kept trying to map out in my mind how all this might be connected. But there were still so many unresolved questions. Antonio Perez, a CNI agent, was the nephew of Miguel Cortez, the head of Grande Distributors. Through my online searching, I learned that Cortez was the son of the businessman who was brutally murdered in El Paso thirty-five years ago, only two weeks after the mysterious plane crash that supposedly killed Joe and his father. Fifty million dollars had possibly been stolen. Maybe this whole thing wasn't a Mexican intelligence operation—maybe it was personal. But then why the hell was the CIA involved? Al Del Luca had been at that meeting with Joe at the Hay-Adams hotel in DC. I'd found nothing else on the man that said his participation was on a personal level. From what all I could gather from online searching, Al Del Luca went to the University of Pennsylvania, where he was on the wrestling team. He was not with Joe, Greta, and Ethan at SMU. So what was the connection?

I sighed and shook my head, which was really starting to hurt from trying to keep all this information straight. And now I needed to somehow put all this out of my mind for a couple of hours while my family properly mourned together.

"You okay?" Taylor asked me.

She stood in the doorway of our bathroom, all set and ready to go, wearing a simple black dress and black heels. Even though there was a clear sadness behind her eyes, I thought she looked beautiful.

"Yeah, I'm fine. Why?"

"You just seem . . . distant."

"Sorry. I just want to say the right things up there today and really honor your dad. It's got me a bit preoccupied."

That part was true. I had agreed to speak today at the service. And I hadn't given myself much time to prepare anything. I'd started making notes only this morning.

"I'm sure you'll do great," Taylor said. "You always say the right things."

"What about you? Are you okay?"

"I think so, actually. I have to admit, watching that video with you last night was really cathartic for me. I think it kind of helped me turn a corner. It reminded me how blessed and fortunate I have been all these years to have a father like mine, who was always there for me. I could always count on my dad for help, for support, for wisdom and guidance. He was always willing to be honest with me. If it wasn't for my dad, I probably wouldn't have this amazing life with you. And I wouldn't trade us and our girls for anything."

I didn't even know what to say to her right now. *He was always willing to be honest with me.* To think that all my countless lies to her the past few days had been to cover up her own father's lies.

But I smiled, nodded my head. "Me, neither. The girls almost ready?"

"Yes. My mom is doing their hair right now. They are excited about getting all dressed up."

"Good. We need to head to the church in about ten minutes."

We arrived at Central Christian Church in the heart of downtown and parked in the back parking lot behind the old Romanesque-style sanctuary building. My mother-in-law seemed to be doing okay, although she wasn't saying much. Olivia and Nicole kept drifting back and forth between giggles about something silly to quiet sadness when no one was talking. I hated that they had to go through this kind of thing at such a young age. I planned to tell a few funny stories about Papa in hopes that my girls would feel some semblance of light on an otherwise dark day for all of us. There were plenty of fun stories about Joe that I could share. Of course, I now also had plenty of stories about Joe that I could never share—and that was weighing me down.

A church administrator named Joslin met us inside the church building in a back hallway and offered us refreshments in a private room. We then made our way into the main sanctuary with its ornate arches, columns, domes, stained-glass windows, and wooden pews. Looking around, I guessed there were already about a hundred people walking down the aisles and finding seats, with many more entering from the front lobby. I checked my watch. The service was scheduled to begin in about fifteen minutes. Pastor Larsen, a tall bald man with a goatee, came over and warmly greeted us. He would be officiating today. We spent the next few minutes mingling with some of the guests, thanking them for coming and accepting their sincere regards.

About five minutes before the service, I told Taylor I wanted one last chance to review my notes. Then I slipped out of the sanctuary into a back hallway and shut myself in the private room with the refreshments. Pulling out a notecard from the inside pocket of my suit jacket, I began to skim through the tiny scribbles I'd made all over it. This was going to be a surreal experience. All the wonderful stories and meaningful things I had to say about my father-in-law were true. But now I knew there would also be a lot left unsaid. I didn't know what awaited me at the end of this pursuit—or if I'd ever reach the end. Nothing felt certain anymore.

I shook my head, tried to focus on my notes. I had only a few more minutes. I needed to be faithful to the matter at hand. For Taylor. For Carol. For my girls. And for the hundreds who loved Joe Dobson and thought so much of him. I needed to set aside the rest of this mess and also be faithful to myself. No matter what I uncovered about my father-in-law, Joe had always been there for me. Taylor was right. My family wouldn't even exist had Joe not guided me back to shore on that fateful day back in college. I could certainly be there for him right now. Taking a deep breath, I put my notecard back in my pocket.

Just as I was about to leave the private room and rejoin my family in the sanctuary, my phone buzzed. I pulled it out, took a glance at an incoming text message. It was an odd phone number. My phone identified it as coming from Mexico City. That made me perk up.

Then I read the brief message and felt my heart jolt.

Alex, please stop looking into my past. You're putting yourself and my girls in danger. Just let me go, son. Please. I'm sorry.
—Bear

My hands immediately started shaking. *Bear* was what Nicole sometimes called Joe. She'd started with *Papa Bear* when she was little and then had shortened it to just *Bear*. She liked to call him that at times, because Joe would often growl like a bear and chase her around until she laughed so hard, she nearly peed her pants. I stared at the text, read every word carefully. *Stop* and *let me go*? Could this be . . . real? Could Joe actually be alive? Impossible. I'd seen the burned van and the body bag with my own eyes. I'd held his charred belt buckle and wedding ring in my own hands. Someone had to be messing with me. But why? How would they know to use the term *Bear*?

Not sure what to do, I called the phone number. It went straight to an automated voice mail. So I texted a quick response.

Who is this?

I stared at my phone screen, waiting for a reply. Nothing happened.
I called the number again. Straight to voice mail.
My heart was pounding now.
I texted again: Please respond.
Again, nothing. No response. I read the text a third time. *I'm sorry* is what Joe had mouthed to me from inside the minivan after those guys had grabbed him. Whoever had sent the text had repeated it. He'd even said *my girls*, which was what he always said when talking about Taylor and my daughters at the same time. My whole body was trembling. I kept telling myself that this could not be possible. Joe was dead. We were about to put him to rest in a matter of minutes. And yet everything within me wanted to believe it.

There was a knock at the door. It jarred me back to reality. I went over, cracked it open, found Pastor Larsen standing on the other side.

"Alex, we're about to get started."

I nodded. "Okay, I'll be right out."

Shutting the door again, I tried to take a deep breath and let it out slowly. I could not go out there and sit next to Taylor in this kind of shape. I had to somehow find a way to calm myself. But how the hell was I supposed to stand up there right now and give Joe's eulogy?

THIRTY-THREE

My hands were still shaking as I returned to the sanctuary and made my way to the very back of the lobby, where my family had gathered. Inside, the pews were almost all filled. The girls were peeking through the closed doors inside the sanctuary. Carol stood beside us, looking somber. I stepped up to Taylor, who gave me an odd look.

"What's wrong?" she asked. "You look pale?"

I knew she'd see it all over my face. "Just . . . nervous."

"You didn't get this nervous even before big football games."

"This feels bigger than any football game."

I tried to take some quick breaths without being too obvious. I thought about the text again. If it really was Joe, where was he? Mexico City? Whose phone was he using? Why not call instead of text? And why no response at all to my returned texts or calls? What the hell was going on?

Taylor reached out and grabbed my hand. She again took a peek over at me. I forced a small smile. Could she feel my fingers shaking? Music was playing inside the sanctuary. Joslin opened the back doors for us. We then followed Carol and the girls into the sanctuary while everyone turned to stare at us with grim faces. Were we about to have a funeral service for a man who was still alive? This felt like an out-of-body experience. I recognized most people in the room from various parts of our personal and professional lives. I did my best to put on a good face. We made it all the way to the front and found our seats in the first row.

After we were seated, the pastor walked onto the stage, stood behind the podium, and warmly welcomed everyone. I couldn't even focus on his words. My phone was on vibrate. I hadn't felt any movement from inside my suit jacket but couldn't be sure. I so badly wanted to reach inside and see if another text had arrived. But I knew I couldn't do that right now.

Everyone stood, including Taylor, who looked down at me with a furrowed brow. I also stood quickly. We'd been invited to sing a hymn. The lyrics were up on a big a screen behind the podium. I kind of mumbled my lips. In a few moments, I was going to be invited onto the stage to give my speech. How was I going to pull it off? My throat felt so dry. I stared down at Olivia and Nicole, who were both wearing black-and-pink dresses. Olivia was trying to follow some of the words, but Nicole was staring off into space. I had to pull myself together for them. I had to do this for Taylor.

The song ended. Everyone sat. Except for me. Swallowing, I took a step toward the stage. My legs felt rubbery. But I kept going. I moved onto the first step, then the second, and then the third. I glanced to my left, where Pastor Larsen sat off to the side. He gave me a reassuring nod. Before turning to face the audience, I looked up at the big screen. There was a photo of Joe on it, wearing one of his sharp business suits. It looked like it had been taken from when he was still running his law firm with Steve Edmonds. I stared at his face and wanted to yell, *What the hell is going on, Joe!?*

Turning, I stepped in behind the podium and faced the crowd. Then I reached into my suit jacket and grabbed my notecard.

"Good afternoon," I began. "My name is Alex Mahan, Joe's son-in-law. And it is a privilege to be standing in front of you today . . ."

I kept talking, but my mind was wandering. Was my voice shaky? I couldn't really tell. I went on to talk about the first time I met Joe and how much he made me feel at home. I told a joke about Joe helping me with my golf game. The audience laughed. The more I talked, the more I calmed down. I kept telling myself that I was going to get through this somehow. I started making better eye contact with the crowd and even smiled at people. I made my way down the story list on my notecard. I was almost there.

As I was nearing the end of my speech, my eyes went to the very back of the sanctuary, where I spotted a woman sitting all by herself in the last row. I looked a little bit closer and suddenly stumbled over my words. Greta Malone. She had on black sunglasses and a black wrap around her head, but I was sure it was her. Why was she here? Would she stay around so I could finally talk to her? I tried to find my place in my speech again. As if sensing me staring right at her, Greta stood, slipped out of the row, and headed to the back exit. I cursed to myself. I couldn't let her walk away. I had to get off the stage right now and go after her.

I cleared my throat, tried to force myself to look really sad, and abruptly ended my speech with, "I love you, Joe. Thank you." Then I left the podium. Instead of returning to my seat next to Taylor, I slipped by Pastor Larsen and found a side exit from the sanctuary. Now out of view, I bolted up the hallway to the front of the church building. Finding a door to the outside, I pushed it open and spilled into an outer courtyard. I looked left and right, trying to find the blonde woman on the sidewalk in front of the sanctuary. But I didn't spot her anywhere. I sprinted forward, followed the sidewalk to the right, where there was a parking lot next to a secondary building. I hustled around to the lot and then paused, looking for any signs of Greta. Where did she go?

I began running through the lot, searching cars, wondering if she could be sitting inside any of them. Not having any luck in the parking lot, I circled the entire church block to see if she'd left on foot. I peered up and down the sidewalk. Cursing, I spun around, couldn't find her anywhere. She had disappeared on me again.

I was sweating something fierce, running around in the hot sun in my business suit. I knew I had to get back inside the sanctuary. Taylor would be wondering what the hell I was doing. I had to be with my wife right now. Moments later, I walked back into the sanctuary and waited until they were singing another hymn before rejoining my family. Taylor gave me another look of concern. I forced a smile to let her know I was fine.

But I was not fine. My already unstable world had just been completely flipped upside down. If Joe might still be alive, I felt more committed than ever to talking with Greta—even if it meant flying back to DC tonight and staking out every campaign event. The woman had answers. And I sure as hell was going to get them.

THIRTY-FOUR

The reception after Joe's service was a complete blur to me. I did my best to engage people on some level, but I was completely checked out. I kept excusing myself every few minutes to find a corner where I could privately look at my phone. I'd sent a half dozen text messages to the same phone number in Mexico City but still had not received any response. At this point, I doubted I would. I felt caught in an emotional tug-of-war. On one side, my head said it was impossible that Joe was still alive. Someone was just messing with me. Someone who didn't want the truth exposed. Could it be Greta? The CIA? On the other side, my heart was begging for it to be true. If Joe was still alive, what should I do? He was telling me I was putting my family in danger. That I should stop my search for answers and let him go.

Could I really do that?

When all the hugs and condolences were finally finished, we climbed back into my Tahoe as a family and drove home. The girls raced up to their bedroom to change clothes and prepare to go to the lake house. The luggage was all packed. All I had to do was get my family turned around quickly and back out on the road. I was eager to do that so I could come up with my own next steps.

Taylor and I returned to our master closet and began changing.

"What happened to you up there?" she asked me.

"I just lost my composure a bit." I knew she would ask me about it. "So rather than break down crying, which I didn't really want the girls to see, I decided to cut my talk short and go gather myself."

"You did really good, babe. My dad would've appreciated it."

"Thanks."

"It's hard to believe it's really time to move on now."

"Yeah. I know."

It's all I could think to say. There was no way I could tell Taylor that her dad might still be alive right now. I had no idea if it was actually true. The only path forward was more and more lies. I felt like I had built a fortress around me and wasn't sure how I'd ever find my way out. Would it ever end?

"Mom was pleased," Taylor added. "I could tell."

"She told me she loved the video."

"Yeah, she wants to watch it again at the lake house tonight."

"How do you think the girls are doing?"

"Really hard to say. There were definitely tears."

I put on a pair of jeans and a T-shirt. I heard my phone buzz on the dresser next to Taylor, where I'd set it down a moment ago. She picked it up to hand it to me. When she did, Taylor glanced at the message.

She looked up at me with a furrowed brow. "Who is Greta?"

I cocked my head, felt my heart jump. "What?"

Taylor handed me my phone, but she did not look happy. When I read the text message, I could see why.

Meet me in Room 314 at the Driskill Hotel at 8 p.m. —Greta

It was a random local number. I wasn't sure how to respond to Taylor. The fact that a woman she didn't know was texting me to meet her in her hotel room tonight after I was shipping my family off to the lake obviously looked suspicious. I had to either tell my wife the whole truth right now, or I had to find a quick way to circumvent disaster. Considering that the truth would lead me down a path to telling her there was a million-to-one shot her dad could still be alive after she'd just found some closure, I decided on my answer.

"I don't know who this is," I said. "I don't know anyone named Greta."

Taylor's eyes narrowed. "Don't lie to me, Alex."

"I'm not. This clearly wasn't meant for me. Why do you think there's no contact info for the number? Or any other text messages between us?"

I handed her back my phone to take a look. She still seemed wary. I needed to take another bold but risky step to get out of this.

"Babe, just call the number," I suggested. "Or text her back. Use my name. See what happens. Because I promise you whoever this is will tell you it was a mistake."

It was a chance I had to take. But I figured there was no way that Greta would actually answer my call or even respond to a text from me. She had given me instructions. I figured there would likely be no other correspondence between us until I stepped into that hotel room in a couple of hours. But would Taylor call my bluff? My wife seemed to consider it for only a moment before her shoulders gradually relaxed.

"Sorry," she said. "It's just . . . I'm an emotional mess right now."

I tried to hide my relief. "I know. Me, too."

Thirty minutes later, I had them all packed up in Taylor's Lexus SUV. I hugged and kissed the girls and my mother-in-law. Then I leaned into the driver's window to give Taylor one more kiss.

"I'll try to wrap this up quickly," I reassured her.

Then I watched them drive away. I had somehow managed to keep myself steady since receiving the text from Greta, but I could now feel a surge of adrenaline overtaking me. I checked my watch. In one hour, I would finally be face-to-face with a woman I was convinced held the answers to this entire thing.

THIRTY-FIVE

I parked in the nearest spot I could find a couple of blocks away from the Driskill Hotel, which sat on one end of Sixth Street, Austin's famous downtown party strip. Because it was Saturday night, live music of all types blared from five blocks' worth of bars, pubs, and hot spots. The closed-off street was packed with a mix of mostly college students and young professionals. I had to weave in and out of the crowd to make my way over to the hotel. Taylor and I had spent quite a few nights out here during our college days, but it had been a while.

Taylor had texted me a few minutes before, telling me they had arrived at the lake house. The girls were already in the hot tub on the back porch. Having them away made me breathe a little easier. If the text from Joe was real and they were truly in danger, I wanted to get them out of town until I could resolve all this.

I still could not wrap my head around the text from Mexico City. *Let me go.* If it was real, did my father-in-law really expect me to drop this whole thing and just let him disappear? And why just the one text? Why no other explanation? I felt really confused. He kept saying he was *sorry*—first while inside the minivan with his captors, then again in the text—which led me to believe he felt he'd brought this whole thing on himself and his family. Had Joe actually stolen $50 million thirty-five years ago? If so, why would he do that? Was that what led to his father and some mystery stranger being killed in the plane crash? I again hoped that Greta Malone could give me some legitimate answers in a few minutes. I wondered why she'd finally stopped running from me and wanted to meet. This was a conversation we could have had several days ago when I'd first called her on the damn phone.

The crowd on the street around me seemed to be growing thicker by the moment. I kept getting bumped because some of them were already wildly drunk. When I came up to the front steps of the historic Driskill Hotel, I paused and checked my watch. I wanted to knock on Greta's hotel room door at exactly eight. I didn't want to do anything that might mess up this opportunity. She had clearly been skittish up to this point. I didn't want her running again. For reasons I still had not yet confirmed, she had a skill set to easily evade my pursuit. I again thought about the old photo of her standing inside the CIA building. Was Greta a CIA agent? Hopefully, I was about to find out.

But before I could take another step forward, I felt something hard suddenly push up against my back, followed by the voice of someone in my ear who now stood uncomfortably close behind me.

"Stay very still, Alex, or I will shoot you on the sidewalk."

I stiffened, felt a surge of panic race up my spine. The man had a slight Mexican accent. Antonio Perez? The CNI agent? I didn't move. I believed he would shoot me dead right there. Could no one else see the gun? We were surrounded by people on all sides of the sidewalk and street. But no one was paying attention.

"What do you want?" I asked over my shoulder.

"We'll get to that. Walk slowly forward, and turn right at this next crosswalk."

I took a few steps forward, gave a quick glance back. It was indeed Perez. My mind started churning. Had Greta set me up? Was she somehow involved with Perez and Joe's abduction? Or was the text telling me to meet at the hotel tonight a fake? Had Perez really sent it? I had no way of knowing at this point. But I certainly didn't like the idea of letting this man take me somewhere outside of this crowded party strip. I had to do something, and quick. I turned right, as instructed. Then I spotted two police officers across the street. I wondered if I could somehow grab their attention. As if sensing my hesitation, I felt the gun jab me even harder from behind.

"Keep moving, Alex. Don't be stupid."

"Like Ethan Tucker."

"That was unfortunate. But yes, he was stupid."

"Does the CNI know what you're doing?"

"Stop talking and just walk."

The crowd was beginning to thin out as we made our way up the sidewalk away from Sixth Street. I was growing more concerned. If I was going to make a move to get away from this guy, I had to do it soon. Once we were all by ourselves, I would have no chance of escaping. I felt my pulse racing. Ahead of us, I noticed a group of five college-age girls, most of whom were already stumbling around, coming down the sidewalk toward us. One girl wearing a black leather jacket, jeans, and heels looked like she was going to be sick and maybe vomit right there on the sidewalk a few feet in front of me. It was the best opening I would probably get right now. Instead of passing by the group without any acknowledgment, I paused and turned to her.

"Hey, you okay?" I asked.

She was now bent all the way over.

"Oh, Jill, don't do it here," one of the other girls said to her.

But it looked like there might not be any stopping her. Jill was already gagging. I felt the gun jab me in the back again. I didn't move right away. Then Jill vomited and spewed everywhere.

Perez jerked back to avoid the spillage. When he did, I took off sprinting up the sidewalk away from him. I ducked into an alley directly behind the bars on Sixth Street, just in case Perez started shooting. My legs were racing forward, as fast as I'd run in a long time, in and around dirty dumpsters, piles of boxes and trash. I spotted several back doors to bars and wondered if I should dart inside one of them. Would the doors be unlocked? Would it be foolish to delay and check? I chose to keep on running, wanting to create as much distance as possible.

A second later, I realized I should've chosen a bar door. Bullets started flying. One hit a metal dumpster only a few feet in front of me. I'm not sure where the other went. But I didn't feel anything, so I didn't think I'd been shot. The gunshots were loud but somewhat muffled, as if Perez had some kind of silencer. Instead of continuing my sprint down the alley and being exposed, I tucked in behind the next dumpster I could find. I couldn't outrun bullets.

How far back was Perez?

I was breathing so damn hard. I had to find another way out of here. A door opened a few feet up ahead of me to my right. Someone stepped out from one of the bars and began tossing trash bags out the back. I took off for the open door. When I got there, I shoved the guy to the side, mainly to protect him in case a bullet was headed our way. Then I burst through the open door into a back hallway leading to a small kitchen crowded with cooks and waitstaff. I didn't slow down. I had to assume that Perez would follow me into the bar. Weaving in and around bar staff, I tried not to knock over anyone else. But I got a lot of weird stares and "What the hells" from them.

Seconds later, I found my way inside the busy venue. It looked like some kind of bar and arcade combo. People were equally crowded around the bar area and the various game stations. A DJ was pumping rock music so loud, I could barely think straight—which I really needed to do right now. I took a moment, ducked in behind a game station, watched the door from the back where I'd just entered. I wondered about my next move. Should I make my way out the front doors onto the crowded sidewalks of Sixth Street again? Or just stay put, hoping Perez couldn't find me?

I had my answer a few seconds later when Perez appeared from the back. His eyes darted right and left. He spotted me before I could duck out. Cursing, I bolted for the front doors of the bar, threading through various groups of partyers, until I burst onto the sidewalk again. When I did, I rammed straight into a huge guy with spiky black hair and a black tank top. He looked like he hadn't missed a day in the gym since birth. And he wasn't at all happy with me. Before I could slip away, he grabbed me by the back of the shirt, started cussing me out. I couldn't believe my bad luck. I was already running away from a deadly assassin, and now I was going to have to fight some meathead?

Before the guy could take a punch, I heard someone next to him yell, "Dude! He's got a gun!" A ripple of panic hit the crowd. That's when Perez stepped up to the muscleman and aimed his gun right in his face. The guy immediately let go of me and put up his hands in surrender. The crowd was scattering and knocking each other over in the process. Perez turned his attention back to me, took dead aim with the gun. I wasn't sure if he was going to shoot me or if we were going to set off by ourselves again.

Neither scenario happened. Instead, I saw Perez's head whip back in a weird way. Then I immediately spotted the hole in his forehead, followed by blood beginning to gush out. Perez's arms dropped to his side, and he fell straight back onto the sidewalk. What was panic before from the crowd now exploded into flat-out terror. Before I could even try to make sense of what had just happened, I felt another strong hand on my arm, followed by a voice in my ear.

"Come with me, Alex! Right now! I'm with Greta!"

I peered up and realized it was Al Del Luca, the CIA agent whose house I'd broken into yesterday in DC. I didn't have time to think. I went with him, up the sidewalk in a tidal wave of other runners, away from the dead man who lay behind me in a growing puddle of blood.

THIRTY-SIX

Del Luca sent me up the elevator inside the Driskill Hotel by myself. He said he wanted to hang around in the lobby and make sure there was no other trouble for us. I just nodded and kept moving. Was the man at all concerned he'd just shot someone dead out there and the police might come looking for him? It was hard to comprehend that a CIA agent had just killed a CNI agent outside on the sidewalk in order to save me. I was in shock. But I was certainly glad Del Luca had pulled the trigger. From the look in Perez's eyes, I believed the man was about to shoot me and be done with it.

Stepping out of the elevator, I moved down the hallway until I finally stood outside of Room 314. I took a moment to gather myself. The woman inside had an odd thirty-five-year history with my father-in-law, starting when Joe still went by Daniel Gibson. I had no idea what to expect when I stepped inside this hotel room with her. But it was finally time to find out.

I knocked, waited. A second later, the door opened, and Greta poked her head out. Recognizing me, she fully opened the door and allowed me inside. The hotel room was a suite with a living room, a separate bedroom, and a balcony. Greta had the balcony door open. I could hear sirens outside. Would the police come looking for me, asking questions? Greta wore a black sweater and black slacks. She walked over, shut the balcony door, and blocked out some of the noise. Up close, she still looked every bit the stunner she was in the old pictures. It was a strange thing, standing face-to-face with a woman who had once been married to my father-in-law.

"Thanks for coming, Alex," she said.

"Well, I've clearly been wanting to talk to you."

"I know. I'll explain. Are you okay?"

I tilted my head. "You know about what happened out there?"

She nodded. "Just got off the phone with Al, my man downstairs."

"Are you CIA, Greta?"

She pressed her lips together, as if pondering where to start. "How about a drink first?"

She went over to a little antique bar cabinet, where she poured herself a glass of what looked like bourbon. She peered over to me with a raised eyebrow.

"No, thanks," I said. "I think I need to be clearheaded for this."

She walked over to a sofa with two chairs. "Let's at least sit down and not be so formal."

She sat on one end of the sofa. I made my way over to one of the chairs and took a seat.

"Where do I start?" Greta said, mostly to herself.

"How about we go back to my first question. Are you CIA?"

"What I'm about to tell you is highly classified information. Not even my husband knows all of this, and I'd like to keep it that way. I *was* CIA. For about twenty years. Operated mostly covertly in the field all over the world under dozens of different names."

Even though I'd wondered, I still felt stunned by that answer. "Is that why I can't find anything about Greta Varner online?"

She nodded. "How did you know my name was Varner?"

I told her about finding the old love letter she'd written to Joe—or to Daniel. And then discovering that she was in college with him at SMU.

"Joe was the reason I went into the CIA," she explained. "He knew it was something I'd wanted to do, but my parents were resistant. He was the one who really encouraged me to follow my heart, no matter what."

"Joe took the photo of you standing on the CIA emblem?"

"Yes. He visited while I was doing my internship with the CIA."

"Only he was Daniel Gibson at the time."

"Correct. Why don't you tell me what you know, and I'll fill in the gaps?"

So I did. I spent the next few minutes telling her everything I'd uncovered, starting with my uncertainty around Joe's financial investment in my company to discovering Ethan Tucker had wired the $5 million to my father-in-law—all the way up to my deadly encounter outside with Antonio Perez. I figured if the guy in the lobby downstairs had been willing to kill a man in my defense, I could trust Greta Malone. But I did not tell her about the text message I'd received earlier from someone claiming to be Joe. I wasn't sure what to do with that just yet. Did Greta already know?

"What happened with that plane crash, Greta?"

"The day that changed *everything*," she mused, sighing and taking a sip of the bourbon. "I remember it like it was yesterday. I went from overwhelming grief to total relief, and then into complete shock."

Greta said that Joe had told her in the days leading up to his trip to El Paso with his father that they had some serious concerns about their client. His dad had grown to believe the businessman was using his company to launder tens of millions of dollars for two different drug cartels inside Mexico.

"They flew down to El Paso that day to end their lawyer-client relationship," Greta said. "Later that afternoon, I got a devastating call from someone at their office telling me that the plane had crashed with both of them inside. I was beside myself with grief but also confused."

"Why confused?"

"Joe had told me that morning he wasn't flying home with his dad. He said he was buying a car from someone there—a 1977 Corvette he'd been searching around for—so he hoped to be driving home in the car. He was really excited about it. Later that night, I heard the door to our apartment open, and Joe was suddenly standing there. I couldn't believe it. He had a cap real low on his forehead and was wearing sunglasses. He quickly shut the door, as if someone might be watching from the outside, and he didn't want to be spotted."

I moved closer to the edge of my seat. I'd been desperate to hear this story ever since I'd read the news article at the SMU library. Greta said Joe told her that the meeting with the client did not go well. The businessman made some threats and basically said it was too late for them to get out—at least alive. Joe's dad reiterated that they would no longer represent them on any legal matters, and they left. Before flying back to Dallas, they stopped off at a diner for lunch, where they met a desperate young drifter who told them he had family back in Dallas that he missed. Joe's dad offered to fly him home.

"So he was the other person on the plane?"

She nodded. "No one ever knew because, like I said, the guy was a drifter. There was no family searching for him after it happened. Everyone just presumed it was Joe. His dad had dropped him off beforehand to buy the car. Joe told me he was certain the plane crash was no accident. He believed someone from one of the drug cartels sabotaged it."

"I spoke with an airport technician who was there that day. He thought the explosion looked more like a bomb had gone off."

"We suspected that. I was thrilled that Joe was alive, but he was a mess. He was obviously distraught that he'd just lost his father. But it was more than that. He was so angry at those who did it. And he felt helpless against them. He knew if he went to the police that nothing would likely ever happen. He couldn't prove a thing, and the cartels had too much influence over the authorities. Plus, he believed that when the cartels got wind that he was still alive, they would come after him and finish the job. So he came up with another plan."

"Steal their money," I interjected.

"Right. Joe said he had access to bank accounts through some paperwork that their client had unintentionally given them. He believed the only way to protect himself and hit back was to take what mattered most to them. Their money. But he couldn't just take it. Joe knew he would need to completely disappear. And he'd need help making sure the money disappeared."

"Ethan Tucker?"

Greta nodded, took a sip of her drink. "Joe and Ethan were best friends. Ethan was already a wiz in the financial field. I called Ethan and told him to get over to our apartment right away. He was as shocked as I was to see that Joe was still alive. Joe told him all that had happened and then asked for his help to wire the money around until no one could find it."

"How much, Greta?"

"Just over fifty million dollars."

I shook my head. I could hardly swallow that figure.

"Joe believed taking the money would not only give him leverage should they ever discover he wasn't really dead, but it might also cripple their entire operation. He wanted me to help him vanish. Because I'd already done my internship with the CIA, I had met some people during my time in DC. We hung out at bars and drank a lot. One guy who constantly hit on me specialized in IDs and paperwork. Joe wanted me to reach out to him and see about getting him a new identity. Said we could pay the guy whatever he wanted to not ask any questions about it."

"So you did it?"

"Yes. One of the hardest things I've ever done in my life."

"Why?"

"Because it meant Joe and I could no longer be together. He knew when the money went missing, they would come to Dallas and ask questions. They would be looking for people who were connected to Joe and his dad. Joe would have to immediately leave town and never come back—at least for a long time. I told him I wanted to go with him, wherever he went—I was his wife, after all—but he wouldn't stand for it. He refused to let me change my own identity, walk away from my family in the dark of night, and put them through all of that pain and misery. He also wouldn't let me give up my dream of the CIA to be on the run with him."

It was hard to imagine what I was hearing. Joe had a good reason for stealing the money and changing his identity—to protect his own life.

"So the plan worked?" I asked her.

"Yes. Joe went to his office in the middle of the night and got the bank account info he needed. We spent a couple of days and got everything together. New IDs, paperwork, wiring instructions. The next day, Joe wired the full fifty million dollars out of his client's accounts, and Ethan began moving it and hiding it. I cried my eyes out when Joe got in the cab and drove away. He didn't even want me to know where he was going. At least, not yet. He wanted to protect me."

"But you sent the letter to Joe in Vancouver only a few weeks after he left?"

"I did. But it was in response to a postcard he sent to me. After he left, I moved to DC right away. A postcard showed up in my mailbox one day. Joe told me he had settled in Canada and was starting over."

"Did you continue to correspond?"

She shook her head. "No. He never responded to my letter. I didn't reconnect with him again until many years later, after the dust had settled. Joe had already gotten married again and had a child."

"Did anyone come looking for you in DC?"

"Yes. A couple of guys followed me around for a few weeks. I could tell they'd been inside my apartment. One tried to pose as an insurance agent wanting to ask me questions about my dead husband. But they were careful with me because I was with the CIA. They eventually left town. I never heard from anyone again."

"What about Ethan?"

"He transferred to his firm's London office right away. As a precaution, I didn't even call him for several months. But when I did finally talk to him, he said nobody ever came around to ask any questions. He felt good about covering his tracks."

"Did you guys stay in touch over the years?"

"Here and there. We all went on with our lives. But we touched base maybe once a year or so. I was surprised when Joe moved back to Texas. I thought it was risky. But he told me about his wife's mother getting sick and how she wanted to be close to take care of her. You know, Joe never touched the fifty million dollars. He just left it alone in various hidden accounts for over thirty years. Not until he pulled from it to help you start your company."

"Are you serious?"

"Yes. He said he just couldn't handle the sad look in his daughter's eyes every time you left for the airport for another business trip."

That revelation took me off guard. Joe had never used the money for himself. He'd only touched it when Taylor and I were in need.

I moved the conversation forward. "So why did the three of you gather in DC two weeks ago?"

"Joe unexpectedly reached out to Ethan and me. And he wanted to talk only in person. So we all agreed to meet. Joe told us he'd run into a businessman from Mexico at a governor's gala back in Austin who looked vaguely familiar. Then he realized the man was the son of their former client from thirty-five years ago. Joe said he remembered that the guy had actually been inside the office with them the day that he and his father had tried to break off their legal relationship and received the death threats."

"Miguel Cortez, head of Grande Distributors."

"Correct."

"Did he recognize Joe?"

"Joe wasn't sure, but that was his fear. The guy kept looking at him funny, as if he did, and started asking a lot of questions. Joe got out of the conversation as quickly as he could and then left the gala right away. But he was really uneasy about the whole thing. He wanted to tell us what had happened and put us both on high alert."

"How did Al Del Luca get involved?"

"Al and I go way back. Spent a lot of years in the field together. Even though I left the CIA to start a new life and have a real family years ago, I kept up with guys like Al. So I reached out and asked him for his help. To look into things for us and see if we should actually be concerned about Miguel Cortez."

"Did he find anything?"

"Yes. Al called me a few days later, said he'd been to Mexico City and had done some surveillance. He said Miguel Cortez was convinced Joe was actually Daniel Gibson. I texted Joe right away, but it was too late. That's when you called me and gave me the horrible news." She sighed. "I told Joe not to go to Mexico."

I shook my head, felt a fresh wave of guilt push through me. "He tried to pull out of it at the last minute. It's my fault that he still came with us. I guilted him into it."

"You can't blame yourself. You didn't know. After I spoke with you that first time on the phone, I was still concerned about your family. So I asked Al to hang around you guys for a bit. Both Ethan and I had planned to stay way below the radar for a while. I wanted to make sure there was *nothing* that tied us back to Joe. But I didn't realize how far you'd go with all of this."

"Wait a second? Are you telling me I led them to Ethan?"

Greta finished off her drink, giving me the answer. I sat all the way back in my seat, pressed my hands to my face, feeling like a thousand pounds of weight had just pressed down on me.

"That's just great," I sighed.

"As you know," Greta continued, "the man who Al Del Luca shot out on the sidewalk tonight worked for the CNI. So he was well versed in surveillance. He may have been monitoring your phones."

"I can't believe I'm the reason Ethan is dead."

"Again, you can't blame yourself, Alex. I should've jumped in sooner."

"Still . . . maybe I will have that drink."

I stood, walked over to the antique bar cabinet, and poured myself a glass of whatever Greta was drinking. Then I took a big swig of it. "So what happens to that guy out there who Del Luca shot? Won't the police start asking questions?"

"We have a way of working these things out."

"*We* meaning the CIA?"

"Yes. Al will also make sure you stay off their radar."

"This is unbelievable. Do you think my family is still in danger?"

"I can't say for sure whether Miguel Cortez will continue to pursue this now that his nephew is dead. We know that Joe didn't tell them where to find the money because he didn't know. Ethan always kept it on the move as a secondary point of protection for Joe."

I walked over to the balcony window. I could see police cars and ambulances and a gathering crowd on Sixth Street below.

Greta got up and stood next to me. "Hey, I want you to know how sorry I am about Joe. And I'm sorry I gave you the runaround this past week. I needed time to figure out what we were dealing with. I have to protect my husband and his potential future in Washington. If any of this leaked out right now, it would likely turn into a big story that could wreck the election for him. I didn't want to risk that happening."

"So why did you come to the service today?"

She let out a deep sigh. "I couldn't stay away. Joe was one of the best men I've ever known. I think a small part of me never really stopped loving him, even after all of these years. What we had way back then, even for a brief moment in time, was really special. I had to be there today to say goodbye."

"Greta, what if I told you that Joe was still alive?"

She snapped her head to look over at me. "What?"

I walked back over to my chair, sat, ran my fingers through my hair.

"Alex?" Greta said. "What are you talking about?"

"I received an anonymous text message from Mexico City right before the service started today from someone claiming to be Joe."

Pulling out my phone, I brought up the message, held it out for Greta. She walked over, took the phone, and read it carefully.

"How do you know this is from Joe?"

"He called himself Bear."

"Bear?"

I explained how Nicole would sometimes call him that.

Greta read the text message again and then handed my phone back to me. "But you said you ID'd him at the scene of the vehicle explosion."

"I did—sort of. The body was too burned to make an ID. But I had his wedding ring and his belt buckle that had been recovered in the fire. Plus, the body type was the exact same as Joe's."

Greta sat on the sofa again. I could see her mind working. "I don't get it. If there is any truth to this, why would they fake his death?"

"I don't know." I knew she was probably just thinking out loud and not really asking me. "Can Del Luca do something to find out if this is real or not?"

She shook her head. "I can't ask him to do that."

"Why not?"

"Look out that window again. Al just shot and killed a CNI agent. He needs to go back to DC tonight and get some separation from this whole thing. Or else he's going to find himself in serious trouble. Like I said, all of this was a favor to me. Nothing was sanctioned by any of his bosses. I can't ask him to go back to Mexico again and start digging around to see if there is any truth to this. For one, I'm not sure I'm really buying it. If this was really from Joe, why wouldn't he give you something more? The message is so brief and lacks any real confirmation. No photo, no explanation, nothing."

"So what the hell am I supposed to do, Greta? Just forget about it?"

She sighed, considered it a moment. "Probably."

"Are you serious? I thought you cared about him."

"Listen to me, Alex. Even if this message was legitimate—and I have doubts about it—after what just happened out there on the sidewalk, Joe is surely dead by now. Or he will be shortly when word of this gets back to Mexico City tonight. If you want to protect yourself and your family, you should probably do exactly what Joe told you to do in that message. *Let him go.*"

THIRTY-SEVEN

I drove home reeling from my meeting with Greta. But I was grateful to finally have the full truth. My father-in-law was not a fraud like I had begun to believe. There was no extramarital affair. There was nothing sinister behind his secrets. Joe had been dealt an extraordinarily cruel set of circumstances early in his life. He'd responded the best way he could think of in what must have been an emotionally charged couple of days after his father had been killed. Unfortunately, the ripple from that response had carried forward for more than three decades before eventually catching up to him.

But I was still left with one daunting question: Where did I go from here? What Greta said made a lot of sense. When word got back to Miguel Cortez that his nephew had been shot and killed, the man would surely execute Joe on the spot *if*—and it was still a big *if*—my father-in-law had actually been alive earlier this afternoon and was the one who had sent me the text message.

Should I do what Greta suggested and let Joe go? Should I forget everything I'd just uncovered this past week, hope this all went away now that Antonio Perez was dead, and try to move on with my life? After all, Taylor, Carol, and my girls knew nothing about any of this. Our friends and family had all just said their goodbyes to Joe and were now beginning the process of healing from the loss. Could I do the same? Could I say goodbye to my father-in-law and bury these secrets forever? Joe had somehow managed to pull it off for thirty-five years. Was I capable of doing the same thing? Should I? I wasn't sure yet.

I pulled my Tahoe into the garage, walked inside my quiet house. It was always odd when my girls were not around. I was so used to hearing the pitter-patter of their little feet on the hardwood floor and the various noises they made while playing, singing, or watching movies. I moved into my home office, fell into my executive office chair, spun around to look at the container that supposedly held Joe's ashes.

Were they his? Someone else's? Would I ever even know for sure?

My eyes drifted over to a framed photo of my father-in-law and me standing together for a photo op on the first tee of a charity golf tournament from this past year. Joe was smiling big with his arm wrapped around my shoulders. The memory was so fresh in my mind, and it wasn't just because we enjoyed playing golf together.

"How're you feeling today?" Joe had asked me.

We were carrying our golf bags up to the fancy clubhouse that was hosting the golf scramble today. The event was being put on to raise money for a local nonprofit called Mobile Loaves & Fishes that served the chronically homeless.

"Back is still a little stiff, but I think I'll be all right."

I had tweaked something in my back two days ago while building a new bookshelf in the girls' upstairs playroom.

"Good. I don't plan on losing this thing today."

We shared a smile.

"I'll do my best," I said.

Setting our golf bags down, we walked up to a table where a couple of women were checking in golf participants. Dozens of guys were standing all around, some taking practice swings, others simply chatting it up before the tournament began. Most of the younger men looked a lot like their older partners. That was because this was a father-son golf tournament, which made me feel a little uncomfortable. But Joe had insisted on us playing together. We waited in line until it was our time to register.

"Names?" one of the gals asked my father-in-law.

"Joe Dobson. This is my son, Alex Mahan."

"Well, son-in-law," I clarified, feeling awkward.

We each got a packet with a sleeve of golf balls, tees, and a towel.

Then Joe pulled me off to the side for a moment. "Listen, I want you to know that I never think of you like a son-in-law. My heart says differently. You are my son, Alex. You became my son the moment you married my daughter. Don't ever think otherwise."

I exhaled deeply, knowing I sat at a crossroads. I could get up, climb back into my car, drive out to the lake house, join my family, and move on with my life.

But would a real son do that? Would he ever let his father go?

I pulled out a prepaid cell phone I'd picked up at Target after leaving the hotel, just in case my own cell phone was being monitored, as Greta had suggested, and called Raul.

"What's with the new phone number?" he asked me.

"I'll explain in a moment. If I give you a phone number from Mexico City, can you trace it?"

"Most likely. What do you have?"

I paused, feeling at a decision point. I either let Joe go right now—which was what he basically had begged me to do—or risk everything in one last Hail Mary effort to see if I could possibly find him alive and bring him home. I thought about Taylor and my girls. If I did this, I couldn't guarantee I'd return to them safely. Anything could happen to me. But I also knew if I didn't do this, I might never be able to live with myself. In so many ways, Joe had rescued me. It was time for me to try to return the favor.

I told Raul about the text message, my deadly encounter with Antonio Perez, and my meeting with Greta at the hotel.

"Will you help me?" I asked him.

"This is still my case, Alex. I have a duty and a responsibility to pursue it to the end. But we must be careful. My investigation into Miguel Cortez and his nephew has been closely monitored by others around here. I have a very bad feeling about it, so I'm keeping things close to the vest. But I will track down this phone number."

"Thank you. If I get on a plane tonight, I can be in Mexico City by early morning."

"I'll meet you there."

THIRTY-EIGHT

I managed to get a seat on an eleven o'clock red-eye flight to Mexico City. Most travelers looked to be asleep within a few minutes of takeoff. I sat by myself in an empty row near the back of the plane and stared out the window into darkness. Although I was physically exhausted, I couldn't sleep. Just like every other night this past week. I wondered if I'd ever be able to get a full night's rest again. If I had to keep lying to Taylor for the rest of our marriage, I doubted it. I had just replied to her good night text, where I'd implied that I was about to get into bed myself. If she suddenly decided to call me, I'd have to decline it and make up an excuse for why I didn't answer her when we talked again in the morning. Could I really live my life like this? I felt sad for Joe, who had felt forced to do this very same thing for more than three decades. I also felt bad for Carol, even though she knew nothing of it. Lies in a marriage build a chasm that can never be bridged until the truth is finally revealed.

The plane touched down at Mexico City International Airport a few minutes after five in the morning. Raul had arrived before me. He told me by text he'd had success tracking the phone number back to an apartment building about thirty minutes from the airport. He was already there, waiting for me in his rental car. In a herd of other early-morning traveling zombies, I went through customs, got cleared, and finally found my way outside of the airport. I had only my backpack with me with a couple of changes of clothes and some toiletries. I had no idea how long I would be in Mexico City but wanted to stay as flexible as possible. After locating a long line of taxis on the curb, I jumped into the first one available and gave the driver the address for the apartment building.

I felt a renewed sense of optimism now that Raul had been able to actually trace the phone number back to a real location. Surely someone at the other end of the phone had answers for me. I hoped they would tell me that Joe was still alive. After about thirty minutes of navigating traffic, I was finally dropped off at the curb in front of what looked like a low-rent four-story apartment building sandwiched between two other similar crumbling structures in the heart of Mexico City. The sidewalks in front of the buildings were mostly empty. The sun had not yet risen.

As I watched the taxi take off, I looked around at a few of the cars parked along the curb. I sent a quick text to Raul, letting him know I'd arrived and asking for his exact location. But I didn't get a response. So I called his phone. Again, no answer. That made me uneasy. I began walking up the sidewalk, peering into the vehicles parked at the curb as I passed by them. No Raul. They all sat empty. I crossed over the street to be on the same side as the apartment building.

Then I noticed a gray Honda Civic with a Hertz rental car license plate frame on the back parked on a side street. It looked like someone's head was peeking over the driver's seat. Circling the rental car to the passenger side, I glanced in and noticed Raul sitting behind the wheel. I opened the passenger door and climbed inside. And that's when I realized something was horribly wrong. Raul's head was actually cocked a bit to the side, a hole near his temple, and blood was flowing down his neck and soaking the collar of his white shirt. I cursed. Someone had just shot him. I felt complete panic push through every inch of my body. Was he already dead?

"Raul?" I said, pushing on his shoulder, accidentally getting blood on my fingers. This only made him slump over farther against the window. I cursed again. Whoever had done this had to still be close by. It had only been twenty minutes since I'd last corresponded with Raul. Were they watching me right now? Were they about to go for a second kill? I had to get the hell out of there.

Glancing down, I noticed Raul's small notepad sitting in the cup holder. I remembered him using the same notepad when I'd first met him. I quickly snagged it, shoved it into my pants pocket. I opened the door and kind of stumbled back into the street because my legs felt wobbly from shock. Then I froze in the sudden headlights of a car that had just pulled straight up to me and stopped. I was blind to whoever was inside. Was it the same person who had just shot Raul? Did they already have a gun pulled on me? Red-and-blue lights started swirling on top of the vehicle, followed by a quick siren chirp.

THIRTY-NINE

Two uniformed officers got out of the police car. Approaching me, one of the officers began speaking rapidly in Spanish. They were both focused only on me at the moment and not yet paying any attention to what was inside the rental car next to me. But could I keep their attention on me? My heart was pumping so fast, I was having a difficult time breathing. I looked down at my left hand, noticed the fresh blood on my fingers in the glow of their headlights, so I squeezed my hand together to try to hide it. This was a disaster. They had just seen me stumble out of the rental car. They were about to find Raul shot dead inside and probably think I had something to do with it. What was I going to tell them? The truth was beyond explanation and would likely get me thrown in jail for a long time. I had visions of rotting away in a dark Mexican prison cell without my family even knowing what the hell had happened to me.

I heard one of the officers say "ID" among a host of other Spanish words. I nodded, slipped my backpack off my shoulder, unzipped a pocket, and pulled out my passport and wallet. I handed both of them to the officer who'd requested it. He was portly and looked to be in his fifties. The other officer was slightly younger but also did not look to be in the best of shape. The officer in front of me shone a little flashlight on my passport and examined it with narrow eyes. At the same time, the younger officer began staring over toward the rental car and slowly started to make his way around to the driver's side. I felt even more panic set in. Everything was about to unravel on me. Not only was my friend shockingly dead, I knew I could very well be accused of the crime if I couldn't find a way to get out of this right now.

But what was I supposed to do? Run from the police?

Swallowing, I decided I had no choice but to run. I couldn't be taken into custody. I would lose any opportunity to find Joe and would quite possibly not see my family again for a long time. At the moment, neither of the two officers had their guns drawn. To them, I supposed it was still just a casual stop to question someone who looked suspicious to them. But I knew within a matter of seconds, this was going to explode into a major crime scene. I glanced left, right, looking for my best escape route. It was probably to my left through the alley behind the apartment buildings.

With all the force I could muster in two quick steps, I moved forward and put my full right shoulder into the portly police officer holding my IDs. Stunned by my sudden attack, he stumbled backward, tripped, and fell to the pavement. Then I dropped my backpack, pivoted left, and took off running for the alley. I heard the two officers yelling at me from behind. I darted into the dark alley a split second later, and for the second time within the past ten hours, found myself sprinting through trash, boxes, and debris while trying to escape someone with a gun.

My foot caught the edge of a box, causing me to face-plant into a muddy puddle. I quickly picked myself up, glanced behind me, but I couldn't see either of the officers. Were they pursuing? At this point, I was probably trying to outrun their radio calls for backup more than anything else. Exiting the alley, I spilled out onto another city street. But I never slowed down. I crossed the street, found the next dark alley, and kept on running. I could hear sirens starting to go off all around me. My legs were on fire. But I didn't stop to catch my breath until I'd probably covered a full ten blocks.

FORTY

I hid in an alley for more than an hour, watching the streets and my back. Based on the sounds of sirens, I felt confident I was outside of whatever circle the police had deemed their search territory. When the sun finally came up, I found the courage to step out into the open again. I couldn't hide in an alley all day. But I didn't stay exposed for long. I quickly ducked into a nearby breakfast diner, where I cleaned myself up in the restroom by scrubbing the mud off my face and the blood from my hand. I also noticed for the first time that I had a big gash under my shirt on my left shoulder, probably from my spill in the alley. Finished in the restroom, I grabbed a booth near the front window of the diner so I could monitor the street while I tried to figure out what the hell I was supposed to do next. Raul was dead. Who had shot him? Raul had mentioned last night he felt like his efforts to investigate Miguel Cortez were being monitored from within. Did someone from his own team take him out before he got too close to the truth?

All I had with me now was what I possessed in my pockets: my phone, a wad of cash, and Raul's notepad. I'd left behind my backpack, passport, and wallet. I had no idea how I was supposed to get out of the country without my passport. But I tried not to focus on that just yet. One step at a time. I'd come here for a reason, and I fully intended to follow through with it. Otherwise, my friend Raul had died in vain. But my only hope at taking a next step was if Raul had written down more specific information in his notepad.

Pulling it out, I began to flip through pages of notes about his various police cases until I came across the last thing he'd written down: *Second floor, #227, Basurto Building.* A wave of relief poured through me. I had to get back over there right away. As I began to slide out of the booth, the sound of a television behind the main counter grabbed my attention. I hadn't paid any attention to it before now because the news anchors were speaking in Spanish. But my head jerked over in the direction of the television when one of the news anchors said my name plain as day: "Alex Mahan." I cursed. My face was on the screen. It was the same image as my passport photo. The word *sospechoso* was on the screen below my photo. I guessed this meant *suspect*, because the next thing they showed was video footage of police and medics surrounding the gray rental car where Raul had been shot. It was jarring to see myself as a wanted man on television.

I noticed the young waitress wearing an apron behind the front counter glance over in my direction. It was time to go. I tried to be casual about slipping out of the diner, but once I hit the sidewalk again, I was moving in a hurry. I spotted what looked like a convenience store across the street from me and headed in that direction. Inside the store, I found a black knit cap and some aviator-style sunglasses among the various food and drink items and took them up to the counter. I had no idea if the clerk would accept US dollars, but that was all I had on me. So I put a fifty-dollar bill on the countertop, hoping that would convince him. He kind of looked at me oddly, so I gave him a shrug as if saying, "Is this okay?" He nodded, took the cash. And he clearly wasn't planning on giving me any change in return.

Before leaving the store, I pulled the black knit cap down on my head and put on the sunglasses, hoping they would provide me some cover out on the streets this morning now that my face was being splashed across TV. Especially because I had to walk right back to the same block of the crime scene where I was now a suspect. I wondered if news like this would somehow make its way back to the States. Could Taylor be watching CNN this morning and suddenly see my face up on the screen? I doubted it, although it still made me uneasy. Had I made a huge mistake coming down here? It certainly felt that way at the moment. I had no choice but to keep going.

Back out on the sidewalk, I hustled to backtrack through the same streets I'd traveled an hour ago and returned to the four-story apartment building. Arriving, I made sure to stay clear of the side street where I could now see several police cars, medical vehicles, TV news crews, and a small crowd of onlookers behind a police barrier. I thought about Raul and shook my head with grief. The man had been so helpful to me. And now he was dead. If I made it out of here, I vowed to make it up to his family somehow.

Head tucked low, I headed up the sidewalk to the front of the apartment building and then slipped inside. Apparently, the elevator wasn't working, as most people were taking the stairs up and down. So I did the same and ascended to the second floor. Upstairs, I found a few young kids playing with toys out in the hallway. One boy was pushing himself back and forth on a scooter. I smiled at him and moved past, my eyes studying the numbers on the outside of the doors. I finally came upon 227. For a moment, I wondered if I should just knock and ask about the phone number. But then I decided against it. Whoever had the phone obviously wasn't interested in talking to me based on their ignoring my phone calls and text messages. Instead, I drifted down to the opposite end of the hallway, where I hung out near the stairwell and pretended to be on my phone. Hopefully, no one would question what I was doing there.

Ten minutes later, someone stepped out of 227. A woman in probably her thirties, wearing a blue dress, black flats, and a big purse over her shoulder. She shut the door behind her and began to head toward me. Could this be the one? Already prepared, I pressed "Call" on my phone and dialed the same number that had sent me the text from Joe. The woman made no movement toward her purse. The phone rang twice on my end before it went to an automated voice mail, which led me to believe someone had pressed "Ignore." It wasn't this woman. I turned my back as she entered the stairwell behind me. Then I returned to watching the apartment again.

It took another thirty minutes before a second person finally stepped out of the unit into the hallway. A teenage boy wearing a black hoodie and jeans. I placed the call, watched the boy. The teenager pulled his phone from his pocket, examined it, pressed a button, and sent my phone call straight to voice mail.

FORTY-ONE

I wondered what to do next. The teenager had the phone that was used to send me the text from Joe yesterday. Should I confront him about it? Or follow him? I decided to follow him. Maybe he would lead me right where I wanted to go. Maybe he would take me straight to Joe. The boy bounced with young energy and descended down the stairwell two and three steps at a time. I had to hustle to keep up while also trying not to be obvious I was trailing him. The teenager hit the sidewalk outside. He paused a moment to place earbuds in his ears and then got moving again. Thankfully, the boy seemed to have no interest in what was happening with all the police cars and crowds off to his left and headed up the sidewalk in the opposite direction.

I followed closely behind him. If this was real, I wondered how a teenager could be involved with Joe. How had my father-in-law gotten use of the boy's phone? Did this kid let him use it? If so, why? I hoped to find out soon. I stayed ten feet back as we both paused at a streetlight and waited for traffic to clear. The streets and sidewalks had quickly grown congested. This was a city of twenty million people, and it seemed as if most of them were out and about right now. A metro bus pulled to the curb, and passengers got on and off. The kid was on the move again, even though we didn't have a "Walk" sign. He eased around the front of the bus and out of my sight for a moment. I hustled forward. When I got to the front of the bus, I saw the kid sprinting across the street. I cursed. Why was he suddenly running? Did he know I was following him?

I took off running after him. The kid was fast. But I was motivated to catch up to him. Everything was riding on not losing the boy. The teenager hit the sidewalk on the opposite side of the street and hustled past a high-rise construction site surrounded by a security fence. Workers in hard hats were out on the sidewalk. The kid easily threaded them. I did the same, like I was back on the football field carving up the defense toward the end zone. We were getting some stares from onlookers. I hoped no one recognized me from the news. I was gradually catching up. The boy was only fifteen feet ahead of me now. Even though I was in great shape, something told me the kid had more stamina. If I didn't find a way to grab him soon, I would run out of gas.

The kid passed a grocery store and then darted into a narrow alley between buildings. I dipped into the same alley a couple of seconds later, nearly turning my ankle trying to keep my balance. I noticed a tall chain-link fence blocking the alley about twenty feet in front of the boy. Did I have him trapped? The boy paused for only a moment, looking left and right, probably for another escape route through a back door or something. I was within ten feet now. Not finding an alternative escape route to his liking, the kid raced forward again toward the chain-link fence. Arriving, he jumped up onto it, grabbed high with his fingers, and began climbing. I had to get to him before he scaled the top, or it was probably over. I jumped up toward the fence, reached up with my right hand, and snagged his pants leg. He tried to kick loose, but I was much stronger. I easily pulled him back down to the ground.

The boy cowered, put his hands up, afraid.

"Take it easy," I said. "I'm not going to hurt you."

But he clearly didn't understand. I pointed to his earbuds, and he took them out.

"Habla inglés?" I asked.

The kid shook his head. I pulled out my phone. I had downloaded a foreign-language app while on the plane that performed verbal translations. Starting the app, I spoke into it. "I'm not going to hurt you. I just need information. Okay?"

The app translated it into Spanish. The kid nodded at me.

"Why did you run?" I asked him through the app.

The kid answered in Spanish, but the app translated to English. "I was afraid. I didn't know why you were following me."

I pulled up a photo of Joe, showed it to the kid. His eyes kind of flashed. Was that a good sign? I then used the app again.

"Do you recognize this man?" I asked.

The kid was hesitant at first to answer. I tried to make it easier for him. From my pocket, I pulled out my wad of cash and held up two twenty-dollar bills. Then I repeated the question. The kid nodded. My heart started racing. This was real. Joe was not the man in the body bag at the scene of the burned minivan. Up to this point, I had been mostly operating on hope. Still, I had to stay focused. I gave the boy the money. He seemed confused but shoved the money into his jeans pocket anyway.

"Where is he?" I asked. "Where did you see him?"

The teenager seemed more open now. "I work over in a warehouse nearby. Loading and unloading and some cleaning. The old man in the photo is locked up in a back room. He's in bad shape. I've had to clean up after him a few times."

With every word of confirmation about Joe being alive, my heart beat a little faster. "Did he use your phone yesterday to send a text?"

The app translated. The boy nodded.

"Why did you let him do that?" I asked.

The boy answered. "We were alone for a few minutes while I cleaned in his room. He offered me one hundred American dollars for just a few seconds with my phone. We almost got busted."

"By who?"

"Guards with guns. There are always two of them outside."

"Where did the man get the money to pay you?"

The boy pointed at his feet, said, *"Zapato."*

I didn't need the app to translate that. It made sense to me. Joe had always kept extra cash beneath the insoles of his running shoes. There had been numerous times we'd been out on long runs around the downtown trail when Joe would suddenly stop, pull off a running shoe, and give money to a struggling homeless man. He carried the cash with him for that very reason. I remembered now that he was wearing his running shoes when he was abducted.

I asked the most important question next. "Is he still alive?"

The boy responded, "He was alive when I left last night."

I felt a new jolt of hope push through my whole body. Joe was still alive. It was hard to believe after everything I'd been through this past week while thinking he was dead. But I had to get to him.

I spoke into the app. "Will you show me?"

The kid vigorously shook his head. So I held up the rest of my wad of cash. Almost $500. Everything I had.

"Por favor," I begged.

The boy's eyes widened at the sight of so much money.

"Just take me to the warehouse, and that's all," I added.

This time, the boy nodded.

FORTY-TWO

We hurried six blocks over to a warehouse center surrounded by apartments and office buildings. Everything felt crammed together here in Mexico City. I stayed very close to the boy out of concern he might make a run for it again, although I doubted he would bolt until he had his hands on the rest of my cash. We stopped at a quiet corner across from the complex. This street was off the main path, so the sidewalk traffic had thinned out. A sign on the building indicated it belonged to Grande Distributors, just as I'd suspected. The warehouse was enclosed by a chain-link fence with sharp wire at the top. Two men wearing military gear with assault rifles stood at a gated checkpoint for entering and exiting vehicles. I figured this was normal around here. Crime was off the charts in this massive city. I looked over toward the actual warehouse building, which was about the size of my local Home Depot. Ten oversize garage-style doors were currently open with dozens of workers loading and unloading a stable of cargo trucks.

If Joe was inside, how would I even get in there to find him? I couldn't just walk up to the guarded gate. I didn't think there was any way to scale the fence, either. Not with the sharp wire on top. I had to find another way. Even if I got inside, I had no idea how I would get past the two guards with guns whom the boy claimed were always outside of the room where Joe was being held.

"Where in the building?" I asked the boy through the app.

He pointed. "Back right corner."

I handed him the cash. *"Gracias."*

"Tú estás loco," the teenager said to me, shaking his head and taking the money. Then he headed off in the opposite direction of the warehouse.

I turned back to the building, wondering what to do next. I had not planned to do this part by myself. I'd expected Raul to be standing here with me with his police experience and his gun at his side. I wasn't Jason Bourne. I knew no martial arts. I'd taken a boxing class once back in college but figured that wouldn't help me much right now. I was just a normal husband and father who ran a software company that made pretty presentations for other companies. I felt helpless and desperate at the moment. Joe was inside. And I felt ill equipped to go in there and get him. But I sure as hell was going to try.

Then I heard a familiar voice startle me from behind.

"Kid is right. You are crazy."

I spun around, found Greta standing there a few feet away. She wore a dark-green hoodie covering her blonde head, black jeans, and gray tennis shoes. It looked like she was carrying a small black backpack. I barely recognized her.

"What . . . what are you . . . doing here?"

I was so shocked, I could barely put a sentence together.

"I changed my mind," she said.

"What . . . Why?"

"I'd never forgive myself if something happened to you, too."

"But how did you even find me?"

"I told you, Alex, I did this for twenty years."

"You've been following me this whole time?"

"Give or take."

"So you know about my trouble with the police this morning?"

"We'll worry about that later, okay? Is Joe in there?"

"According to the boy."

She stepped up next to me, crossed her arms as she surveyed the property. I couldn't believe she was actually standing there next to me. However, I did find something comforting about having a former CIA field agent by my side, even if she was the same age as my own mother.

"Do you have a gun?" she asked me.

"Where would I get a gun?"

She sighed, glanced in both directions up and down the sidewalk, and then pulled up the front of her green hoodie. I spotted two handguns stuck in a tight black vest holster wrapped around a gray undershirt. Pulling one of them out, she handed it to me. "You ever use one of these?"

I shook my head. "Never."

"Well, hopefully you won't have to today, either. Just don't shoot me."

She gave me a quick lesson on how to handle it. I did my best to shove it into the back of my pants without setting the gun off. This was getting more real by the moment.

"The boy told me Joe was locked in a room in the back right corner with two guards always stationed outside."

She nodded. "Let's circle the block and look for another entrance. I'd rather not have to blast my way through the front. If there's going to be any excitement, let's save it for our exit with Joe."

I couldn't tell if she was joking or not. But I followed her across the street and up onto the sidewalk in front of the warehouse center. Then we circled the block while staying sidled up close to the security fencing. The back of the property was nestled next to another warehouse complex that was not secured by a fence. We entered the back of that property until we were completely out of view from the street. Pausing, we took a good look around. There was really no one else within our vicinity. But I was still unsure how we were going to get onto the property. We had not come across an opening anywhere.

"Let's go in through here," Greta said.

"How?"

Greta tugged off her small backpack. From inside, she pulled out a small black bag and unzipped it. The bag was lined with various handheld tools. She selected a pair of what looked like bolt cutters.

"Where did you get all of this, Greta? The guns? The tools?"

"CIA safe house near Catedral Metropolitana."

She said it so matter-of-factly. Like it was normal.

"At least let me do the cutting," I offered.

Taking the bolt cutters, I knelt down and began clipping upward on the chain-link fence until I was able to push both sides away enough for a small crawl space. I allowed Greta to go through first and then followed. We were now inside the secured property. The back of the warehouse building sat directly in front of us. There was no truck activity in the rear, but there were several back doors interspersed among a host of metal dumpsters overloaded with boxes.

She pointed. "That back door right there is probably close to where they are supposedly holding Joe."

"What about the two armed guards?"

"I'm not worried about them."

I looked over at her. "You're not?"

"I'm more concerned with how many more guys with guns will show up if the alarm goes off and how fast they can get there. If we find Joe where the kid said, we take him. If he's not there, we leave immediately. Agreed?"

"He's there, Greta. I know it."

"Let's pray you're right." Greta pulled her gun out from her vest holster, gripped it in both hands in front of her like she knew exactly what she was doing. "Stay close. Follow my lead."

From the fence, Greta hustled toward the back of the warehouse building with me right on her heels. I glanced up away from us and noticed a couple of guys out back near a dumpster, smoking cigarettes. They didn't seem to be paying too much attention. We reached the rear of the building and then scooted closer to the back door where we felt Joe was being held. Greta put her hand on the doorknob and turned. It was unlocked. She then inched the door open slightly, peered inside.

"Kid was right," she said. "There's a back room. Two guys sitting outside of it with assault rifles nearby. They're playing cards."

"Anyone else inside with guns?"

"Not that I can tell. Normal warehouse workers. Are you ready?"

"How do we get past the two guys with assault rifles?"

"Bullets."

I felt my adrenaline surge. Pulling out the gun Greta had given me, I held it in somewhat shaky hands. I could feel my heart pounding. Was I really about to walk into a gunfight? But then I thought about the deaths I'd already encountered this past week. Ethan Tucker. Raul Sanchez. And my father-in-law was next in line if we didn't get in there soon. This was the only way.

Swallowing my fear, I said, "I'm ready."

"In and out," she reiterated.

"Got it."

Greta turned back to the door, opened it, and slipped inside. I moved in right behind her. Rows upon rows of tall metal shelves lined with crates and boxes sat in front of us. Guys running big forklifts moved up and down the rows, retrieving and distributing items. It looked like any normal warehouse operation. But then my attention quickly shifted to the two men sitting right outside of a plain white door with playing cards in their hands and assault rifles leaning next to them. Greta moved right toward them, her gun aimed. They looked up, startled, but before they could even make a move, she fired off two shots. The first one hit the guy on the left square in the forehead; the second did the same with the guy on the right. Both men immediately fell backward. I wondered if the gunshots could be heard with so much loud noise inside the warehouse. But I didn't look around to find out. I was already racing over to the back room.

I flung the door open, stared inside. The man I loved with my whole heart looked up at me from his curled-up position sitting on the floor against the wall. Joe was alive. But he looked worse than I'd ever seen him. His face was badly bruised and broken. He still had on the same T-shirt and shorts as when he was taken the other day, but they were covered in dirt and grime and what looked like dried blood. There was nothing else in the room with him other than a metal tray with food on the floor next to him. My father-in-law was staring up at me, but it was almost as if he thought he was seeing things. He just squinted at me and didn't even respond.

Shoving the gun back into my pants, I rushed over and knelt beside him. "Joe, it's me. Alex."

This made him sit up. "Alex . . . ?"

"Yes, I'm here. But I've got to get you out of here right now."

"But . . . how . . . ?"

"There's no time for that. Later."

I grabbed his arm to lift him up, which made him grimace in pain. This was clearly not going to be easy. I had no choice but to make him suffer through these movements in order get him out of here alive. Yanking him to his feet, I pulled him all the way up. Joe groaned and tightened up on me. Putting my shoulder under his arm, I dragged him toward the door. When I got to the door, Greta poked her head inside. There was a quick expression of relief on her face at the sight of Joe before she turned more serious again.

"We've got to go," she ordered. "We've already got company."

When we stepped back out of the room, I noticed that a few of the warehouse workers had started to wander in our direction, probably wondering what the hell was going on back here. Greta lifted her gun at them and began pointing. When they didn't move right away, she fired two rounds right over their heads. This made them immediately start to scatter. We had Joe out the back door a few seconds later. When I realized he couldn't walk at all, I lifted my father-in-law up over my shoulder to carry him to safety.

Just like he'd carried me for so many years.

FORTY-THREE

We didn't even make it back to the security fence line where we'd entered the property before a green military-style truck screeched around the corner of the warehouse and sped right toward us. I looked over, spotted two guys with assault rifles in the back bed of the truck. They were about fifty yards from us but making up swift ground. They would be on us in seconds.

"We're not going to make it!" I yelled toward Greta.

She turned, surveyed the situation. I tried to pull my own gun out of my pants, but it was too cumbersome while holding Joe. I set him down beside me while keeping my shoulder under his arm to keep him from collapsing. Joe kept grimacing and groaning and seemed incapable of aiding in his own escape. I wasn't going to be able to help Greta in this gunfight. I would have to keep carrying the brunt of Joe's weight.

"Get behind me," Greta said, moving in between us and the approaching truck.

Greta aimed and fired her weapon. Bullets punctured the windshield directly in front of the driver. She must've hit him, because the truck immediately swerved out of control to our left, throwing the two men with rifles out of the truck bed. They hit the pavement hard and slid forward, their rifles flung in different directions. The truck kept speeding forward, where it collided into the security fence beside us and finally came to a stop. The driver was slumped over the steering wheel and not moving. He was probably dead.

I glanced back toward the other two men in the parking lot. They appeared to be badly hurt. One was still lying face-first on the pavement. The other was trying to pick himself up off the asphalt but grasping his leg. Before we could make our next move, another truck carrying more armed men sped around the same warehouse corner.

"What now?" I asked Greta, feeling panicked.

Greta yelled, "Get into this other truck!"

We hustled over to the truck next to us. Greta yanked open the driver's door, reached inside, grabbed the driver, and pulled him out onto the concrete. He hit the ground with no resistance, clearly dead. I dragged Joe around to the other side, opened the passenger door, did my best to shove him up into the front seat of the vehicle, and then climbed in beside him. Greta was already behind the steering wheel, shifting the truck into reverse. The second truck came to a stop about thirty feet behind us. Gunshots started going off, and bullets started hitting the back window, shattering it. I pulled Joe down in front of me, causing him to yell out in pain, and then I slumped over the top of him to try to avoid being shot. Greta barely flinched. Instead, she punched down the gas pedal hard and thrust our truck backward right at the other truck. We rammed straight into the front of the other vehicle. It jarred me around inside the truck and made my head hit the side window hard. I was dizzy for a moment. Joe grunted in my arms.

Greta then put the truck into drive, stomped on the gas pedal again. We rocketed forward. I heard more gunshots going off behind us and could hear bullets popping through the metal all over our truck. Greta kept swerving left and right, trying not to give them a good target and bouncing us all around inside the cab. We were picking up more speed. I looked over and noticed that Greta's right arm was bleeding. Had she been shot?

"Alex . . . ?" Joe muttered, trying to look up at me.

"Stay down, Joe," I said to him.

"Brace yourself," Greta said to me. "And hold on to him!"

Greta was not slowing down to make the turn to go back to the front of the building. Instead, we were headed right at the security fence again. I could see a busy city street on the other side of the fence. We were going to burst right through it to get out of here. I did what she said and braced for impact while wrapping both arms tightly around Joe.

The truck easily ripped right through the chain-link fence. We bounced hard across a bumpy sidewalk, and then Greta yanked the steering wheel right as we slid into the street. Cars swerved to avoid our unexpected entrance and began crashing into each other. Our truck nearly turned over before finally settling again with all four tires back on the pavement. Greta punched down on the gas pedal again.

I glanced out our bullet-shattered back window. The truck following us was stuck behind all the wreckage. I took what felt like my first breath since I'd put eyes on Joe.

Within minutes, we were deep into the city.

FORTY-FOUR

Thirty minutes later, we were inside a private medical room on the first floor of a nearly abandoned office building somewhere in the dark recesses of Mexico City. Greta acted like she knew the place well. Using her CIA connections, she'd pulled in a local doctor, who immediately started tending to Joe's many wounds. My father-in-law looked even worse under the fluorescent lights. They'd beaten him badly this past week. But he was alive, and that was what mattered most at the moment. Still, where did we go from here? I was a suspect in a crime I hadn't committed. The police officer who'd been working with me was dead. And Miguel Cortez was still capable of causing havoc for all of us. We weren't out of the woods yet. I knew I couldn't just call Taylor right now and give her the good news about her father. This thing was beyond complicated. But Greta seemed to be developing a plan. She was currently on her phone outside of the room, working on a way to get us all out of Mexico City.

Alone with Joe, I stood next to his medical bed and waited for him to open his eyes. The doctor had been pumping him full of pain meds for the past few minutes. Joe had been pretty much out of it ever since we'd dragged him to freedom. I noticed he was finally stirring awake. Joe squinted up at me, his eyes slowly adjusting to the bright light above him.

"It wasn't a dream," he said to me. "You are here."

"I'm here, Joe. You're okay. You're safe now."

His eyebrows pinched. "But . . . what about the girls? Taylor? Carol?"

"Yes, they are okay, too. They are safe back in Austin."

"Thank God," Joe said, exhaling deeply, his shoulders relaxing. "Who is with you? I saw someone else. A woman?"

"Greta," I replied. "She's right outside."

Joe's face wrinkled up. "But . . . how?"

I grabbed a stool, slid it over, and sat. "It's been one hell of a week."

I proceeded to tell him everything that had happened from the moment the minivan sped off with him inside with that black hood over his head. Hearing about the death of his friend Ethan Tucker made Joe tear up and rub his face with his hands. Then finding out I had almost died on the streets of Austin and a police officer had been killed this morning because of this situation seemed to hit him even harder.

"I'm so sorry, Alex. I never dreamed any of this would happen."

"Listen, Joe, I'm okay. You're okay. That's what matters right now."

"Does Taylor know you're here?"

I shook my head. "She doesn't know about any of this."

"Carol?"

"No. I've kept it from both of them. To protect them."

Joe sighed, clearly trying to absorb it all. "I have hated keeping Carol in the dark about this all of these years. But I could see no other way to fully protect her. I always believed the more she knew, the more danger she would be in if this ever unraveled on me like it did this past week." He looked over at me. "I'm sorry you've had to lie to Taylor to protect me. I never wanted my lies to infest the whole family."

"You're alive, Joe. That's what matters right now. What happened after they took you? Why did they fake your death?"

Joe licked his cracked lips. "I had no idea they faked my death. When they finally pulled the hood off my head, I stared straight into the face of Miguel Cortez. That's when I knew for sure what this was about: money and revenge. I tried to convince him that the CIA was protecting my family. I knew enough of the language because of Greta to make it sound convincing. I was terrified he would try to use you and the girls as leverage against me. I guess my bluff worked, and he decided to be more cautious. They put me in another van and drove me for what felt like forever until they shoved me into that dark room. I have no idea where we are right now or even what day it is anymore."

"It's Sunday. We're in Mexico City."

He nodded. "I can't believe you're here. And I'm still alive."

"They've been beating you?"

He swallowed. "Yes. Repeatedly. Cortez wanted answers about the money. He wanted to know who else was involved. He wanted to go after everyone."

"Did you tell him anything?"

Joe shook his head. "I knew he was going to kill me anyway. I was willing to die with the truth if it meant protecting my family and friends."

"I'm glad it didn't come to that. Why did you send me the text yesterday?"

"I overheard men outside my door talking specifically about you. I could tell one of them was Miguel Cortez. That's when I realized you were searching for answers about me and how dangerous it was for you and the girls if you didn't stop. I felt desperate. The boy came in later. I gave him the cash in my shoe and sent the text. But you clearly didn't listen to me."

I gave him a small smile. "Yeah, sorry about that."

Joe started to chuckle but then began coughing.

"Take it easy," I encouraged him.

He reached over and grabbed my hand. "Thank you, son."

I squeezed his hand, fought back tears.

At this point, Greta entered the room and walked over to stand next to me beside Joe's bed. He looked up at her, and they shared a quiet moment.

"You look like hell, Joe," she said.

"Thanks for coming, Greta."

"Yeah, well, I needed a vacation anyway. And I've always liked Mexico."

They both smiled. Greta was no longer wearing her hoodie. She was in her gray T-shirt. I spotted the white bandage wrapped around her right arm.

"Are you okay?" I asked her, nodding toward the bandage.

"Flesh wound. I've seen much worse."

"So what do we do now?" I asked her.

"A team is coming to get us. They'll be here in about an hour. They'll take Joe back to Brownsville and allow him to walk himself into a hospital there, where he'll tell the authorities he just escaped from his abductors. Joe will know *nothing* other than he's been kept in a dark room somewhere near Matamoros the past week, where they've beaten him up real good. You understand me, Joe?"

He nodded. "I understand."

"What about Miguel Cortez?" I asked.

She looked over at me. "We will take care of Cortez privately."

"*We* meaning . . ."

"Yes," she answered, clearly knowing I was asking about the CIA.

"What about me being suspected of a crime here?"

"We'll handle that, too."

"What does that mean?"

"It will go away."

"What? Like it never happened?"

"Yes, all of this will go away. Like none of it ever happened."

My mouth dropped. "You can really do that?"

"You'd be surprised."

"So, what, we just go back to our lives in Austin?"

"Correct. And never tell a soul about any of this."

"Will we be safe?" Joe asked her.

Greta nodded. "I'll keep some guys around you for a little while, just to make sure of it. But I doubt you'll see any trouble once we handle Cortez."

Something told me that Miguel Cortez was not going to be officially arrested. But I didn't ask any further questions. I didn't want to know what *take care of Cortez privately* really meant.

"What about the money?" Joe asked. "I don't even know where Ethan put the rest of it."

"We'll find it," Greta said. "Although I doubt you'll be getting it back. The agency often plays by 'finders keepers' rules."

"They can have it," Joe replied. "Believe me, I never wanted it to begin with. I'm glad to be free of that burden. But why are you doing this, Greta? You're risking way too much."

Greta sighed, pressed her lips together. "Because if I'd have jumped in sooner, Ethan might still be alive. I have to live with that regret, but I won't make the mistake again, even if this ends up causing issues for my husband."

"I'm grateful to you," Joe said.

Greta leaned down, gently kissed him on the forehead. "Rest up. We ship out of here shortly. You have a long journey ahead of you."

Then she walked back out of the room.

I shook my head. "She really is something else, isn't she?"

"Yes, she is," Joe said.

"So I guess we're supposed to keep this secret between us?"

Joe looked up at me with wet eyes. "Listen, son, that's up to you. No matter what Greta said. I've already made my bed. I love Carol. I want to protect her from all of this. I still think it's for the best. But I would never ask you to do the same thing with Taylor. You have to make that decision for yourself."

FORTY-FIVE

A man in a black suit who identified himself simply as Bob walked me straight through Customs at Mexico City International Airport and put me on the first American Airlines flight back to Austin. No questions asked by anyone. It was a surreal feeling being back on a plane headed home after everything I'd just experienced in Mexico City. Joe was alive and safe. I couldn't wait to see the explosion of joy come from my family when they received the shocking news. My girls would have Papa back. Taylor would have her dad. And Carol would have her husband again. Everything in my life could go back to normal, if I wanted it that way.

I thought about what Joe had said to me earlier. He felt like withholding the truth from Carol continued to be the best way to love and protect her. Did I feel the same?

This time, I slept hard on the flight. An airline attendant had to stir me awake after we'd landed around eight that evening in Austin. Once back in my Tahoe outside of the airport, I texted Taylor to let her know I'd finally wrapped things up with my client and would be headed out to the lake house shortly. She "hearted" my text and responded that the girls insisted on staying up to greet me. It felt so strange holding on to information that I knew was about to flip her world upside down in such a deeply meaningful way. But I had no choice. I had to follow the plan. I quickly stopped by our house, showered, put on fresh clothes, and then jumped back into my vehicle.

Forty minutes later, I pulled in front of the lake house. I sat there a moment, taking several deep breaths. It was hard to believe I had ended up here after everything that had happened this week. I felt an overwhelming sense of gratitude. The plan was set to roll out the moment I sent a text to Greta, letting her know I'd arrived. At some point tonight, Joe would call Carol from the hospital to break the news, and the dominoes would begin falling from there.

One more deep breath. One more prayer of thanks.

Then I typed Here, sent the text, and went inside.

We were huddled around the kitchen table, playing a board game with the girls, when Carol's phone finally rang on the counter. I glanced over, noted it was an area code for South Texas, felt chills race up my back. I handed the phone to my mother-in-law. I had been looking forward to this moment ever since I'd pulled Joe out of that dark room earlier today.

"Hello?" she casually answered.

Then she suddenly stood, her chair falling backward. "Joe . . . ?"

Taylor looked over at me with a wrinkled brow. I shrugged.

Carol covered her mouth with her free hand. "Is it . . . really . . . you?"

"Mom, what is it?" Taylor asked her.

"I can't believe it," Carol said, tears suddenly flooding her eyes.

"Nanny, what's wrong?" Olivia asked.

Then Carol yelled, "I can't believe it!"

Taylor stood, concerned. "Mom! What?"

My mother-in-law looked around at all of us with a smile that began to stretch across her whole face. "Joe is alive! Papa's alive!"

We scrambled to pack up everything so that we could drive down to the border as fast as possible and be reunited with Joe. No one wanted to hang up the phone with him, so they just kept passing it back and forth to each other for a while. My girls were laughing and singing. Carol was dancing through the house. Taylor was damn near floating. I did my best to play my part, too, hugging everyone, laughing along with them, and celebrating the overwhelmingly good news. Joe and I even did a great job of faking it on the phone together.

I was changing my shirt in the master bathroom because Nicole had spilled her orange juice on me in the celebration when Taylor walked in to find me bare-chested in front of the mirror.

"You ready?" she said.

Her smile was back. I was so happy to see it again.

"Almost. Just getting changed."

Her eyes narrowed. "What happened to your shoulder?"

I glanced down at my left shoulder, where a white medical patch covered the gash I'd gotten while running away from the police in Mexico City.

"Oh, I was in the garage this morning and tripped over Nicky's scooter. Slammed my shoulder hard right into my toolbox."

"Ouch," she said, stepping up beside me. She gave my shoulder a little kiss. "Maybe I can make it all better later."

She smiled again. I knew what she meant. But I couldn't smile back. I just stood there feeling my insides suddenly twist up in absolute agony.

"What's wrong?" she asked.

"Uh . . . nothing."

She tilted her head. "Babe? Tell me."

I turned to Taylor, swallowed. I loved this woman so much. I knew now what I had to do. We had made a covenant with each other.

I took her hands in mine. "I have to tell you something."

"What?"

"The truth."

"What . . . truth?"

I shut the bathroom door, locked it, and then turned back to her. I asked her to sit down on a stool that was in front of the vanity. I took a deep breath, let it out slowly, and then told her *everything*—starting with the strange text from someone named Greta the night Joe had been abducted and culminating in Greta's help rescuing her father earlier today. Taylor took it all in with wide eyes, mouth open, and repeatedly exclaiming "What?" with every new and stunning revelation. I wasn't sure how she would process the shock, disappointment, anger, and relief that were hitting her all at once. Reliving it all over again still left me feeling breathless.

She ran her fingers through her hair. "I don't . . . I don't even know what to say."

I knelt in front of her. "I'm so sorry I kept the truth from you. I didn't know what else to do. I was trying my best to balance my own shock and desperation with my desire to somehow protect you and the girls from all of this."

She looked up at me, eyes still wide, mouth agape. "I can't believe any of this. Everything I thought I knew about my life . . . has all been . . . upended."

"I know. Please don't be mad at me."

Her eyes softened. She put her hands to my face. "Mad at you? How could I possibly be mad at you, Alex? You just risked your life to go save my father. He's only alive *because* of you and everything you did the past few days."

"Well, he's my father, too."

We embraced and kissed, and I felt five days' worth of heavy burden release from my entire body. The tension I'd been carrying in my neck and shoulders finally relaxed. It felt so good to let it all go. I never wanted that brutal chasm between Taylor and me again.

"My mom really knows *nothing*?" she asked.

"She only knows about Greta, and even that is limited."

Taylor exhaled. "I think my dad was right to shield her. My mom is not wired like me. She's emotionally fragile. I'm not sure she could've handled it."

"Right or wrong, I know he did it out of love."

She nodded. "What do I do now? This is completely overwhelming. I mean, I'm angry at my dad. But I also understand why he did it. I need time to process it all."

"We have a five-hour drive ahead of us."

"Then what? I walk in there to see my dad and act like I'm clueless?"

"I think you'll know when we get there."

FORTY-SIX

Around five hours later, I finally pulled my Tahoe into a nearly empty parking lot in front of the Valley Regional Medical Center. Even though it was well after midnight, Olivia and Nicole were filled with so much energy and excitement that their seat belts could hardly contain them. Carol had the biggest smile permanently etched on her face, and it seemed like all the color had come back into her cheeks. My mother-in-law had clapped and sung songs with the girls the entire drive down to Brownsville.

Sitting beside me, Taylor was also smiling but was still somewhat subdued. I could tell that the wheels had been spinning in her head the entire way. I had no idea what my wife planned to do when she walked in to see Joe for the first time. But I trusted that whatever decision she made would be the right thing for her and her dad. And for us as a family.

Parking in a row up close, we all jumped out of the vehicle. We had to call after the girls to keep them from running inside the hospital without us. But Carol wasn't too far behind them. I'd never seen my mother-in-law move so fast. Walking up to the main doors, Taylor reached over and grabbed my hand. We already knew that Joe was on the second floor, so we rushed into a waiting elevator and pushed the button. I noticed my mother-in-law checking her makeup in the reflection of the elevator door. My girls were like pogo sticks, bouncing up and down inside the elevator. I felt the need to remind them that Papa was not in the best condition.

"Girls, be sure to go easy when you see him, okay? Papa has got a lot of bumps and bruises. So no jumping on him, or you might hurt him. And don't be too scared if he has bandages all over him."

They both nodded.

Carol leaned over to me and Taylor. "Joe told me the doctor said he has five broken ribs and a broken clavicle. He's going to have to take it easy for a while."

"And his face is really beaten up," I added, trying to prepare her.

Carol tilted her head at me.

"That's what Joe said on the phone," I clarified.

Taylor gave me a sideways look. This might be harder than I thought.

When the elevator door opened, Olivia and Nicole rushed out first. We all tried to hurry to keep up as they raced past various nurses and doctors on the floor while searching room numbers for Joe's room. Olivia found it first, burst right inside, followed by Nicole and Carol. I immediately heard a raucous reunion commence inside the hospital room.

"Papa! Papa!"

"My girls!" Joe was even louder than the girls in his exuberance at seeing them.

Taylor paused for a moment right outside the door and squeezed my hand even harder. She turned to me, her eyes already wet.

"Hey, I love you," she said.

"I love you, too, babe. You ready?"

She nodded. We walked into the room together. In spite of my warning, both of my girls were already up in the bed with Joe, who had them wrapped in his arms. Carol was leaning over him and kissing him on the face. Tears were flowing down her cheeks. There were several butterfly bandages on Joe's face, but he looked a hundred times better than he had when I'd left him earlier. It was surreal to think that I had carried him over my shoulder to safety just over twelve hours ago. As the girls wiggled all around him, my father-in-law grunted in some pain, but he never stopped smiling. I'm not sure any of us would for a while. Joe had been dead. And now he was alive again. That truth held up under any version of this event. We could all celebrate it.

Spotting Taylor inside the doorway, Joe held out his arms to his daughter. If Taylor had walked into the room with any reservations, she immediately let go of them. My wife raced over to her dad, fully embraced him, and buried her tear-soaked face into his chest. Joe wrapped his arms fully around her. Watching my father-in-law hold his daughter like that made me tear up. Soon all of us were on top of him, one big family group hug that threatened to suffocate Joe. I gradually pulled Olivia and Nicole back, but we all remained huddled closely around his bed.

"Papa, tell us how you escaped," Olivia said. "I want to hear the story."

"Yeah, Papa," Nicole chimed in. "Did you have to jump off roofs and out of buildings like Aladdin?"

We had explained to the girls that Joe had not died in the car crash, like we had all thought, but had instead been taken by some mean men who probably wanted Papa's money. And that he'd been held somewhere until he was able to courageously escape earlier today. I was concerned that this bit of truth might still be traumatizing for them, but it seemed as if the joy of the moment trumped everything else. I was grateful for that.

Standing at Joe's bedside, Taylor took her father's hand in hers. "Yeah, Dad, tell us what happened. You said on the phone you probably crawled the length of a football field."

"That's right," Joe replied, then looked at the girls. "Maybe even farther."

"Wow," the girls both said in near unison.

With Taylor on one side of the bed, Carol on the other, and my girls still in his lap, Joe began to tell a story of being held captive in a barn not too far from the village, and how it had taken him several late nights to dig a hidden hole with his bare hands before he'd finally managed to crawl out today without being discovered. It was clear that Joe had rehearsed this story and covered all the angles. There were a lot of details that would need to hold up over time. Olivia, Nicole, and Carol hung on his every word.

I glanced over at Taylor. She gave me a subtle smile. She'd made her decision.

And I knew everything was going to be okay.

ABOUT THE AUTHOR

Chad Zunker is the Amazon Charts bestselling author of the David Adams series, including *An Equal Justice*, which was nominated for the 2020 Harper Lee Prize for Legal Fiction, *An Unequal Defense*, and *Runaway Justice*. Chad also penned *The Tracker*, *Shadow Shepherd*, and *Hunt the Lion* in the Sam Callahan series. He studied journalism at the University of Texas, where he was also on the football team. Chad has worked for some of the country's most powerful law firms and has also invented baby products that are sold all over the world. He lives in Austin with his wife, Katie, and their three daughters and is hard at work on his next novel. For more information, visit www.chadzunker.com.